OHIO
DOMINICAN
UNIVERSITY™
SINCE 1911

EYES LIKE WILLY'S

EYES LIKE WILLY'S

By JUANITA HAVILL

HarperCollins *Publishers*

ACKNOWLEDGMENTS

I would like to thank my brother, Denis Havel, who made available to me his encyclopedic knowledge of European military history. He not only served as an enthusiastic and excellent resource person, but also offered relevant and inspiring suggestions for further reading. Interpretations of the information are, of course, my own, but I am deeply grateful for his help.

Many years ago, when I began my research, I contacted Dr. William Wright, founder and first director of the Austrian Culture Center at the University of Minnesota. I would like to thank Dr. Wright for providing me with a list of resources that helped me narrow my search.

My appreciation of used book stores, public and university libraries, and library loan programs in Arizona is limitless. Thanks to them I found diaries, letters, and memoirs written by those living during the period I wrote about, as well as the work of historians who look back on the events and offer their interpretations.

I am grateful to my husband for welcoming Guy, Sarah, and Willy into our lives.

Eyes Like Willy's

For information address HarperCollins Children's Books,
a division of HarperCollins Publishers,
1350 Avenue of the Americas, New York, NY 10019.
www.harperchildrens.com

Library of Congress Cataloging-in-Publication Data
Havill, Juanita.
Eyes like Willy's / by Juanita Havill.–1st ed.
p. cm.
Summary: While vacationing over the course of several summers in Austria, French siblings Guy and Sarah Masson become best friends with a German boy, until the outbreak of World War I puts them on opposing sides.
ISBN 0-688-13672-9 — ISBN 0-688-13673-7 (lib. bdg.)
[1. Best friends–Fiction. 2. Friendship–Fiction. 3. Brothers and sisters–Fiction. 4. World War, 1914–1918–Fiction.] I. Title.
PZ7.H31115Ey 2004 2003014954
[Fic]–dc22 CIP
AC

Typography by Joe Merkel
1 2 3 4 5 6 7 8 9 10
⌘
First Edition

To my companions on the journey,

Susan Pearson and Melanie Donovan

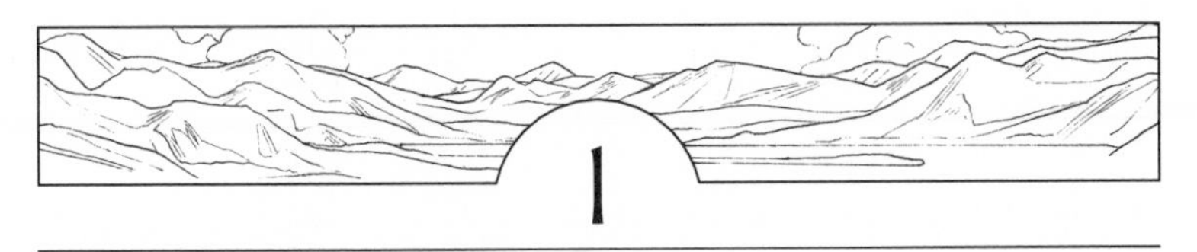

1

SUMMER HOLIDAY: 1906

Every summer in the month of August, Guy and his family left Paris on holiday. When his little sister, Sarah, was a baby, they visited Grand-maman in her big stone house on a farm in Normandy. After Grand-maman died, they traveled to the seacoast for vacation or to the mountains. But the summer that Guy was ten, they rode the train all the way from Paris to a small village in Austria on the shores of Lake Constance. One of Papa's customers, an Austrian, had told them that they must go to Bregenz one summer, and so they did.

It was a long trip. They ate their meals in a dining car on the train, and slept in bunk beds that folded down above their seats in their compartment. After the midday meal, when Maman and Papa had fallen asleep, Guy and Sarah slipped out of the compartment and set off to walk the length of the train. As they neared the car at the end, the train rumbled louder and plunged into darkness. Sarah screamed and clung to Guy's arm.

"Don't be afraid, Sarah. We're going through a mountain. On the other side is Switzerland." He tried to sound brave, but the gloomy chill made him shiver.

Sarah wouldn't let go of Guy until the train reached the end of the tunnel. They blinked in the bright daylight.

"I hope there aren't any more mountains or tunnels," Sarah said as they trudged back to their compartment.

"Of course there will be mountains—and lakes. Papa said that Austria is a country of mountains and lakes."

"I don't mind the lakes," Sarah said.

They slipped back into the compartment where their parents still napped. Sarah picked up her doll.

"Sophie, your bonnet has come untied." Sarah adjusted a small straw bonnet on the doll's porcelain head and tied it in place with a blue satin ribbon. "Were you scared, Sophie, when we went through the tunnel?" Sarah hugged her doll.

Guy checked his suitcase to make sure his model sailboat was safe. The boat, a gift from his father, left little room for his sketch pad and pencils, even though he had dismantled the blue sail and rolled it up beside the boat.

"I'm going to race *Zéphyr* on the lake," he told Sarah. "Papa says my boat will sail faster than all the others, and I think he's right."

At last the train approached the village station. Guy looked out at the lake in the distance. It was like the sea, much vaster than the pond in the Bois de Boulogne where he sailed *Zéphyr*. At the station, Guy wanted to bound from the train and run to the lake to launch his boat and watch it skim across the surface.

"Sarah, please gather Sophie's things," Maman said.

"Guy, let's go fetch a cab," Papa said. He turned to Maman. "Adrienne, we shall meet you there." He pointed to a line of benches in front of the station. Papa liked for everything to be organized, at his publishing business, at home, and even on vacation.

Half an hour later they had loaded the horse cab and squeezed onto the seats, and off they went. They arrived at the hotel and inspected their rooms—a sitting room, three bedrooms, and, at the end of the hall, a bathroom they shared with other guests. It was not nearly as grand as their apartment in Paris, but the flower pattern on the wallpaper and the lace curtains reminded Guy of home.

The next morning, even before they had completely unpacked their trunk, Guy persuaded Maman and Papa that what they all needed most was a stroll by the lake. Guy clutched *Zéphyr* under his arm and trotted off ahead of them.

"Wait for me," Sarah called. "I want to see *Zéphyr* go in the water."

Guy paused for Sarah to catch up; then they headed toward a crowd of people at the lakeshore. Model boats were already floating on the lake by the time they joined a group of children launching their boats. As soon as *Zéphyr* touched the water, the blue sail swelled, and it glided swiftly ahead of the others. Guy tingled with pride when he heard a murmur of awe from the people in the crowd.

"Steady, *Zéphyr*, steady. That's it. Now faster, faster," he whispered as he tried to follow on shore.

Sarah clapped. "Your boat is the fastest, Guy!"

But then a sleek boat with a red sail skimmed right

beside *Zéphyr* and sped ahead. Speedy as she was, *Zéphyr* couldn't catch up with the red-sailed boat. Even before Guy could reach the pier where the boats were headed, the race was over.

"Not fair." Sarah groaned.

"Of course it's fair," Guy said. "Fair and square. The red one is faster, that's all." Guy tried to sound more cheerful than he felt. Still he couldn't help admiring the red sailboat.

"Let's find out who the boat belongs to." Guy ran to the pier to fetch *Zéphyr*. A black-haired boy was reaching toward the red sailboat. Guy rushed toward him, but a man stepped into his path. Guy tried to avoid the man, lost his balance, and crashed into the boy. Both of them toppled into the lake. Splashing, they regained their footing in the shallow water. The black-haired boy was laughing so hard that his eyes crinkled shut. Then he opened them. They were a warm brown color and almond shaped.

"He has friendly eyes," Sarah whispered to Guy when he climbed onto the bank. "He should be mad at you for knocking him into the lake." She stepped back from Guy and brushed at the water spots he was dripping on her dress.

Sarah's right, Guy thought. The boy's eyes glowed like stained-glass windows with sunlight shining through them.

The boy stood holding his boat until Guy had retrieved *Zéphyr.*

"Ich heisse Willy." The boy held out his boat to Guy.

"Vill-ee," Guy repeated, admiring the boat. "My boat is *Zéphyr,*" he announced, and held up his blue sailboat.

The boy laughed. Then he said in French, "Willy is *my* name, not my boat's."

"Oh." Guy smiled. "My name is Guy." He repeated the hard "g" sound followed by "ee."

"I'm Sarah," Sarah blurted out as the boys exchanged their boats.

Willy made a little bow. "A pleasure to meet you, Mademoiselle Sarah." Then he turned back to *Zéphyr.* "Your boat is a beauty, Guy."

"And yours is very speedy. Would you like to sail *Zéphyr*?"

"Yes, very much, but"—he looked down at his dripping clothes—"I'd better change first."

Guy had forgotten that he was soaked to the skin.

"Me too." He gave Willy's boat back to him. "Let's meet this afternoon, here at the lake."

"Splendid."

On the way back to join their parents, Sarah asked, "What are you going to tell Maman?" She stared at his soggy clothes.

"I'll tell her we met Willy."

2

GAMES: SUMMER 1906

How could you, Guy?" Maman was not pleased to see Guy's water-soaked clothes.

"If you knew you were going to jump in the lake, why didn't you put your bathing suit on?" Papa asked.

Guy tried to explain as they walked back to the hotel. "I'm sorry, Maman, Papa. It was an accident."

"He tried hard not to bump into a man who walked right in front of him," Sarah said.

"But then I bumped into Willy."

"Willy?" Maman asked.

"Our new friend," Guy said.

"You have a friend named Willy? I'm delighted you've met a playmate, children. There will be plenty of time for playing, Guy–later. This afternoon we shall all attend to unpacking, and when you have finished, Guy, you will stay in your room and think about how to avoid accidents."

"But, Maman."

"There is no need to protest, Guy."

"Yes, Maman."

All afternoon Guy arranged and rearranged his books, his tin soldiers, and his drawing pencils. He set up the chess board on a little table by the window. He didn't feel like playing himself, and Sarah was still busy helping Maman. He looked out the window to watch the people passing by. Many were dressed for the beach. Girls had shed their dresses for shifts to swim in. Boys wore one-piece swimming costumes. Some of the children carried pails and little shovels. He noticed one boy in short pants, a white shirt, and cap. The boy was hurrying toward the lake and carrying a model boat.

Guy thrust his head out the open window and shouted, "Willy!"

Sarah burst into the room. "Willy? Where's Willy?" She held Sophie in one hand and Sophie's white pinafore in her other hand. She ran to the window and called out, "Hello, Willy!"

"He's too far away to hear us."

But Willy had stopped walking and turned to look in their direction.

"This way, Willy! Up here." Guy grabbed Sophie's pinafore from Sarah and waved it out the window, flapping it up and down and then in circles.

"Don't drop it, Guy!"

"Look. He's coming this way. He sees us." Guy watched Willy wend his way through the vacationers until he stood beneath the window.

Guy shouted down, "Willy, I can't come out this afternoon."

"The wet clothes?" Willy asked. "My mother was resting and didn't see me when I went back to change. Can we meet tomorrow morning then? I'll come by for you, now that I know where you're staying."

"Yes. I'll be ready, with *Zéphyr*."

"Me too," Sarah shouted.

After Willy left, Guy turned to Sarah. "But you don't have a boat."

Sarah shrugged.

The next morning at breakfast Guy announced, "I plan to sail boats with Willy at the lake this morning."

"I hope you're not planning to jump into the lake again today," Maman said.

"No, I won't. I promise," said Guy. He could tell that Maman was teasing.

"This Willy, he's the boy you met yesterday?" Papa asked.

"He's the one with the red sailboat that's faster than *Zéphyr*," Sarah said. "And I'm going with Guy."

Guy frowned. "You haven't even asked Maman."

Sarah turned to Maman with a pleading look.

"You may go too, Sarah, but stay with your brother," Maman said.

"Guy, I expect you to look after your sister," Papa added.

Sarah clapped her hands.

"What a lot of commotion at breakfast!" Papa said. "Are we going to meet Willy before you go galloping along the lakeshore with him?" Papa asked.

"Of course," Guy said.

After breakfast, when Willy came, Guy introduced him to Maman and Papa.

"Excuse me for not speaking French very well," Willy said.

Papa answered in German. "On the contrary, your

French is very good. We are, after all, in your country. With study and practice, Guy should be able to learn your language."

"Is this the boat that won the race yesterday?" Maman asked.

"Yes, Madame. My great-uncle made it for me. He's an officer in the army."

"Your uncle is very clever."

"You should see how fast it goes," Sarah said.

"Please, Maman, Papa, excuse us," Guy said impatiently. "The morning will be gone, and we will still be standing here talking."

"Impetuous boy," Guy heard Papa murmur as he and Willy hurried to the lake. Sarah followed close behind.

The boys took turns sailing each other's boats. Sarah sat on a bench watching. Then she got up and ran along the shore to cheer the boats.

"Willy," she asked, "what's your boat's name? I don't know how to say it."

"*Goldadler*. It means golden eagle."

"Golden eagle," Sarah repeated. "How beautiful!"

Goldadler was always ahead of *Zéphyr*, except the few times it tipped over.

"*Zéphyr* is more stable," Willy said to Guy.

"*Goldadler* is faster," Guy said. Then he asked, "Do you come every summer?"

"Most summers, yes. Sometimes we come for two whole months. The fresh air is good for my mother. She isn't well and needs to rest a lot. We live in Vienna the rest of the time."

"This is the first time we've been here," Sarah said.

"Sarah, we have to persuade Maman and Papa to come back next year."

"Oh, we must," said Sarah.

Willy smiled, and his brown eyes gleamed.

They sailed boats until the sun was overhead and it was time for lunch.

"It's time to go back," Willy said. "I'll meet you tomorrow morning. I can't come out this afternoon. I have to practice piano and flute."

"But it's summer holiday," Guy said.

"Mutti says that musicians don't need a holiday."

"My father says that everyone needs a holiday," Guy said.

"You must be very good, Willy. Please play for us some time," Sarah said.

"I'm playing a little recital for friends of my parents Friday afternoon," Willy said. "Bring your parents too, and you can stay for tea. *Bis morgen.*"

"Bis morgen," said Guy.

"See you tomorrow," said Sarah.

Maman and Papa were pleased with the invitation. On Friday they all went to the hotel where Willy and his parents were staying. Sarah tugged at Guy's elbow. "There's Willy's mother," she whispered as they sat down in straight-back chairs in the salon.

Guy saw a woman standing near the piano. She wore a long white dress and her black hair was pulled back in a bun. She took the arm of the man beside her, a sturdy man with thick brown hair. When she smiled, Guy recognized Willy's smile.

Guy liked listening to Willy play the piano. He was excellent. But Guy felt sorry for his friend. Willy had to play for over an hour. None of the adults seemed to mind, but Guy got tired of sitting still. Finally they had tea, and the cream puffs were worth all of the sitting still. Guy had never had such sweet whipped cream before.

Early the next morning, even before breakfast, Willy made a surprise visit. His father came too, apologizing to

Maman and Papa for coming so early.

"But Willy would like for Guy and Sarah to see the lake," Herr Schiller explained.

"It can't wait," Willy said.

Maman looked from Willy to Guy and Sarah. "Perhaps we all should go," she said.

While the children raced ahead, Maman, Papa, and Herr Schiller strolled after them. Guy reached the lakeshore first. At least, he thought it was the lake. A cloud of mist hung above the water like a curtain.

"It's beautiful," Sarah said.

"So mysterious," Guy said. "A pirate ship could be sailing out there ready to attack."

"And no one would see them until it was too late." Willy slashed at the air with an imaginary sword and made whooshing sounds.

Sarah jumped, but when she saw that Willy was teasing, she frowned at him.

For a while they remained on the beach, watching the mist rise above the surface of the lake.

"From right where we're sitting," Willy said, "the lake is at its longest. Vati told me that it's such a great distance, if you stare out over the lake you can see the curve of the earth."

For a moment the three gazed silently at the invisible distant shore.

Suddenly Sarah cried out, "I see. I see lots of curves."

"Those are waves, Sarah," Guy said, laughing. He couldn't take his eyes off the wide shimmering water.

In the afternoon Willy showed Guy and Sarah a path in the woods behind the hotel.

"Let's play soldier," he said.

They ran deeper into the woods and took turns hiding and stalking each other.

"Did your great-uncle fight in any battles?" Guy asked Willy.

"Oh yes. He was a cavalry officer, you know, on horseback. I'm sure he was brave. He doesn't say much about fighting. Sometimes all he talks about is dancing at fancy balls."

"Did he ever kill anyone?" Sarah asked.

"Sarah!" Guy scolded. Actually, it was a question he wanted to ask himself.

Willy answered, "I'm sure he has. He's a soldier.

That's what soldiers do."

Guy and Sarah met Willy almost every day of their summer vacation. On sunny days they sailed boats and played soldier in the woods. When it rained, they played chess or listened to Willy practice. Whether sunny or stormy, the days sped by.

"Soon we have to go back to Paris," Guy said.

Willy frowned. "And I have to go back to Vienna. I won't see you for a whole year. That's too long to wait."

"Then don't go back to Vienna," Guy blurted out. "Come and stay in Paris with us. You could come to school with me, couldn't you? And we'll sail our boats in the pond. Of course, it's not as big as the lake. We'll take you to the zoo. Have you ever been to a zoo?"

"A zoo? No, I haven't, but I would love to see wild animals." Willy's eyes flashed for a moment. Then he looked down and shook his head. "My parents will never let me go to Paris with you for a whole year."

"Oh, they will!" Sarah spun around. "They will!"

"And if they don't," said Guy, "we will have to do something about it ourselves."

3

THE TRUNK: SUMMER 1906

"I know you've become good friends," Papa said when Guy asked him if Willy could come home with them. "But we have only just met Willy and his parents this summer. Willy is too young."

"Willy is only three months younger than I am," Guy protested.

"What Papa is saying is that you are both too young," Maman said. "We wouldn't let *you* leave us for such a long time, even to live with friends."

"Perhaps when you both are older, young men, you can invite him," Papa said.

"Older?" Guy was disappointed. "I'm talking about now."

But Papa said there was no question.

Guy complained. "I already mentioned it to Willy. He's probably asking his parents right this minute. If they say yes, and I have to tell him the whole thing's off, he'll be crushed."

"Impetuous boy," Papa said.

"You should have waited, Guy," Maman said. "I'm sure Willy's parents will understand."

Guy knew what Willy's parents would say. Parents always seemed to think the same way. Even if they spoke different languages, they thought in the same one—the language of grown-ups.

Guy was not surprised when Willy told him that his parents wouldn't let him go.

Three days before Guy and his family had to travel back to Paris, it rained, and the three friends sat in Guy's room staring out the window in a gloomy mood.

Maman came in to suggest that they organize their packing. She had the trunk brought to the room.

"Why do we have to pack now?" Guy asked. "When I do something before it's time, Papa calls me impetuous."

"Guy, you know that's not the same. I'll leave you to it," Maman said as she left the room.

"Impetuous Maman!"

Guy turned to the trunk. Instead of packing his clothes in it, he hopped into it himself. "We have plenty of time to pack. Climb aboard, mates, and we'll go out to sea."

The trunk held all three of them, although they couldn't move around much, the way pirates ought to when they fight.

"Land ahoy!" Sarah climbed up onto the side of the ship. "It's an island."

"Let's drop anchor here." Guy said. He had tied a curtain cord around his shoe and lowered the makeshift anchor into the sea.

"Come, mates," he shouted, stepping out of the trunk. "What a fine ship she is!" He looked back at Willy, who was crouched in the corner. Guy lowered his imaginary sword and stared at Willy as an idea formed in his mind. "You're coming with us, Willy."

"Of course I am. We have to bury the treasure."

"I'm not talking about pirates, Willy. I mean Paris. You're coming with us in the trunk."

Willy looked puzzled.

"But, Guy," Sarah reminded him. "Maman said never to put the lid down when we play in the trunk or we'll suffocate. How will Willy breathe?"

Sarah had a point. Guy thought quickly. "We'll drill holes in the trunk. Except we'll need a tool to make air holes."

"I don't think it will work." Willy didn't sound enthusiastic. "I'm not so sure we should try it." Willy hesitated, but finally he ran back to his hotel to fetch a tool that he used for making mast holes in his model boats. They took turns drilling air holes in the back of the trunk.

"Not too many," Guy said. "Or it will look like a chunk of Gruyère."

Willy looked up. "How will I eat? Should I bring food?"

"We'll save food for you, from our meals. When Maman and Papa are napping, we'll sneak it to you," Guy said.

"I should bring some biscuits anyway."

"If you want to, but no smelly cheese. That would give you away."

When they finished drilling, Willy climbed in the trunk to try it out.

"You have lots of room," Sarah said.

"I won't when the trunk is packed." Willy scrunched into the corner, his knees bent to his chest. He stared up at Guy with worry in his brown eyes. "I don't know. Maybe we–"

"Of course it will work," Guy interrupted. "Bring what you need and we'll pack it with our things tomorrow."

The next day Willy brought a coat, cap, two books, a folder of sheet music, and his flute too. The only way Guy and Sarah could make enough room for everything was to wear more clothes than they usually did.

The morning they were to leave, Guy wore two shirts, two vests, a jacket, and two pairs of short trousers. He felt uncomfortable, all puffy and warm, but he had no choice. Sarah wore her bathing shift and two petticoats, with one pinafore under her dress and one over it.

Guy pulled some shirts aside and a pair of boots to clear a place for Willy. With everything ready, Guy and Sarah sat down to wait.

"Willy's late," Sarah said. "Something's wrong."

"He'll be here soon. I wish you wouldn't fret, Sarah. Just like we planned, he'll come to say good-bye. Then he'll sneak back up the stairway in the back."

Maman bustled into the room. She held a folded shawl and a hatbox. Guy rushed to the trunk and sat on top of it.

Maman looked around to see if they had finished packing. "Are you finished already? I must say, Guy, this holiday has done you good. You've finally put some meat on those bones. You too, Sarah, you're much rounder, and you've got such rosy cheeks."

She approached the trunk and waved Guy to get off. "Do you mind? I've completely run out of room. I'm sure I can find a nook in your trunk."

Guy slid slowly off the trunk. "But, Maman, if you open the trunk now, you will never get the lid closed again," he said.

Maman raised the trunk lid. "Guy, look at all the room in the trunk!" She dropped the folded shawl in one corner and set the hatbox down on the floor. "It's not level enough for the box. I'll have to rearrange it." She reached into the trunk to pick up a folded coat.

"Let me help you." Guy leaned over the trunk.

But Maman had already lifted the coat up. Underneath it was a cap. "Guy, this isn't your cap. Where did you get it?" she asked.

"Willy gave it to me."

Maman handed Guy the coat and cap and stared down at the open trunk. For a moment she studied its contents. Guy held his breath and turned to Sarah, who was biting her lip.

Maman reached into the trunk. "Did Willy give you his flute too?"

"Guy! Sarah!" Papa shouted from the hall. "Willy has come to say good-bye." Papa ushered Willy into the room.

"Splendid," Maman said. "Now you can give Willy his cap and flute back, and any other of his possessions you have packed in the trunk."

Willy's puzzled stare went from Maman to Guy to Sarah and back to Guy.

In silence Guy took the rest of Willy's things from the trunk and handed them to Willy. Then Maman packed her items and left the room with Papa.

"I'm sorry, Willy."

"It's not your fault," Willy said. "I was coming to fetch my things anyway. I can't go with you. I want to very much, but I can't. Mutti would be too upset if I left for a whole year."

"A whole year," Guy repeated.

"What will we do without you for a whole year?" Sarah whined.

Guy couldn't think of anything cheerful to say.

4

TOGETHER AGAIN: SUMMER 1907

If Willy were with us in Paris, we would take him to the zoo and show him the giraffe," Guy told Sarah.

"And the counting pony, the one that does sums. Remember, Guy, we saw him by the Champs de Mars. He taps his hooves to count," Sarah said.

"He doesn't really know how to count and do sums, Sarah. His owner has trained him. But you're right. Willy would like him."

"And the Eiffel Tower too. We would take him to see it." On sunny days Guy could see the tip of the tower from their balcony window. Grand-maman had taken him to the Universal Exhibition when he was four, and she had grumbled when she saw the Eiffel Tower. "When are they going to tear that monstrosity down?"

But Guy liked the iron tower that reached up into the sky over the Champs de Mars, and he wondered if Willy had seen anything like it in Vienna.

"If Willy were here . . . " Guy and Sarah said often. "If Willy were here, it wouldn't be so dreary."

That winter it was cold and rainy, and it even snowed. Guy wrote letters to Willy almost every week. Willy wrote back, but it wasn't the same as being together. Guy included sketches in his letters to show Willy all of the things he and Sarah wanted to show him. Guy drew pictures of Willy too, over and over, until he made a portrait that he liked.

"It looks just like him," Sarah said, "especially the eyes."

By the time February arrived with a hint of spring, the subject of summer holiday came up every week. Guy began packing the trunk a month before school ended. Sarah was as eager as he was to leave for vacation.

At last Guy's family arrived in the village, and the friends were together again. They swam in the lake and hiked in the woods. Guy and Willy sailed their boats. Guy had made improvements to *Zéphyr*. Now both boats sped along side by side. When the boys ran along shore though, Guy was always ahead. He had grown taller during the year, and so had Sarah. Willy was not much taller than she was now.

One rainy day, Guy and Willy set up Guy's tin soldiers on the chess board. They staged battles that Napoléon had fought: Iéna, Wagram, Austerlitz. Guy chose to fight only the battles that Napoléon had won.

"I want to play with you," Sarah said.

"There aren't enough soldiers," Guy said.

Sarah picked up Willy's flute and began to blow screeching notes on it.

Willy jumped up from his soldiers and took the flute from Sarah. "Here, let me show you how," Willy said, and played the notes of a scale, expertly and clearly.

"Not a flute lesson, Willy. Not now," Guy said.

"Why not? I'm tired of battles. And anyway, Napoléon didn't win every battle."

"Napoléon was a great general, the greatest France ever had."

"Then why did he lose?" Willy said. "Maybe we should do the battle of Waterloo."

Guy began to clear the board. He carefully put his

soldiers away in a wooden box. "I suppose we could play chess."

"And I will have a turn too," Sarah said.

"Anything but the flute," Guy murmured. He let her challenge him to the first game. He was serious about winning, but even with Willy's help, Sarah checkmated him.

"Good game, Sarah," he said, trying to be a good sport despite how he hated to lose.

Losing didn't bother Willy. "Hurrah for Sarah," he said, and, "Hurrah for Sarah," he said again when she beat him twice in a row.

5

RESCUING DAMSELS: SUMMER 1907

After several days of rain and chess and tin soldiers, the sun came out. Guy and Willy took swords they had made from sticks, hung scarf capes over their shoulders, and set off for the forest. Guy loved the way his feet sank softly into the thick blanket of pine needles. The smell of pine was fresh and sharp. He pretended he was on horseback–a noble knight on a quest. He and Willy rode together in search of adventure. If they came upon a dragon, they would kill it. If challenged by enemy knights, they would fight to the death.

"Beware, Sir Guy," said Sir Willy as they rode through shafts of light that pierced the dark, damp forest. "I fear danger lies ahead."

They came to a clearing where an army of fierce knights surrounded them. Shouting, they plunged into battle. They whacked and stabbed, clunking their swords against the arms and legs and weapons of an enemy only they could see. They were careful not to strike a horse. Only evil knights would harm a horse. They beat back their attackers and then all was silent. Until–

A piercing cry sounded. A scream. A lady was calling for help!

"Do I hear the cry of a damsel in distress?" Sir Willy asked.

"Fear not, milady. We arrive to rescue you," Sir Guy added.

They rushed to a beech tree and looked up to see Sarah standing on one branch and clinging to another above her.

"Good heavens, Sarah! How did you get up there?" Willy asked.

Sarah was not in a playful mood. Her voice trembled. The branch she held shook. "It was so easy to climb up, Guy. But I don't know how to come down. I'm afraid the branch will break."

Guy dropped his sword. "Willy, give me a boost."

He put his foot in Willy's clasped hands and grabbed the lowest branch. He climbed onto it and then made his way to Sarah, four branches above him.

"Guy, this branch is so shaky. Be careful."

"You be careful." Guy steadied Sarah as she made her way slowly to the trunk. He held her arm and she climbed down to the next branch. Then, by herself, she descended branch by branch. Just as she reached the lowest branch, her foot slipped. She sat down hard on the branch, then fell backward. She tumbled toward Willy, who caught her, and then they both fell down.

Willy got up and helped Sarah to her feet. "Are you all right?" he asked, and pulled a twig from Sarah's hair.

Guy dropped down beside them.

"I'm fine," Sarah said. "You saved my life, Willy."

Willy put his arm around Guy's shoulder. "Have you forgotten your brother and his act of courage?"

"After all, Sarah, I scaled that tall tree for you. Have you no gratitude?" Guy teased.

"You're very brave too, Guy, but it's not the same," Sarah said. "You're my brother." She looked straight at Willy. "I'm going to marry Willy. He'll be my husband."

Willy's face reddened as if he'd just run a race.

Guy didn't feel embarrassed by what Sarah had said. He thought she had a splendid idea. Someday he and Willy would be brothers.

6

ZEPPELINS AND AN EMPEROR: SUMMERS 1908 and 1909

"You'll never believe what I saw!" Willy stopped to catch his breath.

Guy and Sarah had just gotten out of the cab in front of their hotel when Willy rushed to greet them. His face was flushed from running, his dark hair tousled by the wind, and his eyes shone like pebbles in a sparkling stream.

Guy waited while Willy greeted Maman and Papa.

"What did you see, Willy? Is it still there?" Guy asked.

"Can you show us now?" Sarah took a bag that Maman handed her. "Maman, Papa, we'll unpack later, please."

"Oh, it's gone," said Willy. "We can't see it now, but I couldn't wait to tell you."

"Tell us what?" Guy said.

While they unpacked, Willy told them about the zeppelin he had seen flying over the lake. "I've seen hot-air balloons before, but the zeppelin looked more like a submarine. Instead of going deep in the ocean, it flew above the lake."

"It's filled with hydrogen, isn't it?"

"Oh yes, the hydrogen makes it lighter than air, and up it goes. Count von Zeppelin makes them. Well, he's made one or two. He lives near the lake someplace. I think in Constance, and a lot of people think he's a bit crazy. I don't know if he's crazy, but wouldn't you love to fly in a zeppelin?"

"Can we? Will it come back?"

"I don't know if they take people up in it yet. And anyway, they have to repair it. It fell in the lake and they had to drag it to shore. That's what the newspaper said."

"It sounds dangerous to me." Sarah's eyes widened. "I don't want to go up in the air and fall in the ocean."

"It won't hurt to look at it," Guy said.

They scanned the sky over Lake Constance every day, hoping to see the zeppelin, but there was no sign of a flying sausage. That's what it looked like in the newspaper article Willy had cut out to show Guy and Sarah.

Although they never saw a zeppelin that summer, they spent a lot of time talking about flying machines. When it came time to leave, Willy was so disappointed that Guy tried to cheer him up.

"We'll make our own zeppelin," he promised Willy. "Next summer we'll fly."

When he was back in Paris, Guy spent hours drawing designs for zeppelins. He sent his designs to Willy, who wrote long letters with suggestions. Papa made suggestions too when Guy showed him the designs.

"Interesting, Guy, but I think you should leave the hydrogen flying machines to Count von Zeppelin. Too dangerous. The gas that fills them is flammable when mixed with oxygen, and your mother and I would not like to see you blow yourselves up. Nor would Willy's parents, I'm sure."

"What if we made a giant kite?" Sarah said. "Couldn't we hold on to a giant kite and then someone would hold on to the cord so we wouldn't fly too far away in the sky?"

"A kite? I don't know. Willy has his heart set on a huge zeppelin." Guy realized as he spoke that Papa was right. He knew that he could find motor fuel to power the airship, but where could he get the hydrogen to fill it?

Maybe they should start small. "Instead of a kite, we could make a glider, one with wings."

They arrived in Bregenz the summer of 1909 prepared to build a flying machine. With Papa's help Guy had found thin dowels of lightweight wood, and Maman had donated a pair of old threadbare sheets.

Willy brought cords and ropes and begged a couple of Mutti's silk pillowcases. "Silk is perfect for the wings," he told Guy.

"I'm sure you're right," said Guy, "but that's not enough for a big glider."

Together the three studied Guy's designs. Some of the gliders looked like umbrellas, box kites, or bat wings. They settled on a design with two wings. Each wing was four meters long and a meter and a half wide and would be made of cloth attached to a wood frame with curved wood at the tips. One wing above the other, they were joined by sticks. The one who piloted the glider would hang from two wooden poles attached to the frame of the lower wing. The pilot could swing his legs up and stretch out flat with his feet on a strip of wood behind him or dangle with the poles under his arms.

Assembling the glider plane was much harder than

they thought. Guy knew that the wood had to be light or it would never get off the ground. But they had to be careful when they fastened the sticks together because the wood was fragile and could snap in two easily.

They worked for a week. Sarah kept saying that she didn't believe it would ever fly, but she tacked the sheets in place and worked as hard as Guy and Willy. Another week passed. The work would have gone faster if Willy didn't have to practice every afternoon.

"It's impossible to skip practice, especially piano. Mutter told me she plans for me to play an important recital at the end of the summer, but she won't say any more. I think she's trying to trick me into practicing."

Finally they finished building the *Golden Zéphyr.* They named their craft after their two sailboats, which seemed like children's toys to them now. Papa and Maman and Willy's father came to the beach to watch them launch the craft. Papa and Willy's father stood on either side of Guy, who was in the pilot's cage. The grown-ups helped support the craft to keep it from tipping right or left. Willy held a rope tied to the front and Sarah also clung to a rope from behind. Off they went, running, trotting, jogging, while Willy pulled on the rope.

When Papa and Herr Schiller released the glider, it coasted a few moments in the air, then sank to the beach, where Guy trotted, struggling to keep the craft upright. Again and again they tried, until Willy's father ran out of breath and Papa admitted they were not going to get it any higher this way.

"Go jump off a cliff!" a bystander from the crowd of bathers shouted.

"That's a rude thing to say," Sarah said to Guy and Willy.

"No, he's right," Guy said. "He's giving us good advice."

"He does have a point," said Willy's father. "Perhaps, Guy, you and Sarah can search for a gentle slope somewhere. I'm afraid that Willy has some practicing to do."

Willy frowned, but Sarah was curious. "Can you tell us, Herr Schiller, about the recital?"

With a little smile and shake of his head, Willy's father said, "No, but you'll find out soon enough what it's all about."

Guy and Papa tethered the craft to a bench along the walkway, where Sarah and Maman agreed to remain and keep an eye on it. Without Willy or his father, Guy and

Papa searched for higher ground. They trudged up a winding road past the monastery to the church beyond. They stood near the cemetery beside the church and stared at the rooftops and garden plots below, far below.

"This is surely high enough," said Guy. "Let's go get the glider." A current of excitement rushed through his body.

Papa shook his head. "This is too high, Guy." He pointed to the trees below them all along the slope. "It wouldn't take much wind to blow the glider into one of those trees. It would be wrecked."

Guy shrugged. "What do we do now?"

"Keep searching," said Papa.

They returned to the lakeshore and eventually found a spot where the land sloped down to the lake. It wasn't exactly a cliff, but the slope was steep and Guy was willing to give it a try.

The next morning Papa came with them to help. This time they didn't need anyone to run beside the glider to support it. Perched right above the dropoff, the glider would be airborne as soon as Guy stepped over the edge. Guy grasped the poles underneath the craft. Sarah held up the tail, and Papa and Willy stood below the slope on the beach and pulled on the rope attached to the front.

Guy felt the air lift the craft gently at first, then with more force. Little by little the glider rose. The ground sloped away from his feet, and the glider flew straight above the shore, two feet higher. Guy tried to stretch out and rest his feet on the wood strip at the back, but by then he was sinking toward the shore. He knew he would have to run as soon as his feet touched the ground. But the glider pulled him forward so fast that he toppled to his knees and let go of the glider. It bounced ahead of him three times before he could catch up to stop it.

"You flew, Guy. You were flying!" Sarah shouted. "I want to try it."

Willy and Guy set the glider upright. "We have to make sure it's safe, Sarah, before we can let you fly," Guy said.

"Actually," Papa said, "I think your airplane needs some repair before anyone flies."

"Willy's next," Guy said.

"After we fix it," Willy said.

The next day, after they had replaced two balsa-wood shafts and a torn pillowcase, they returned to the slope.

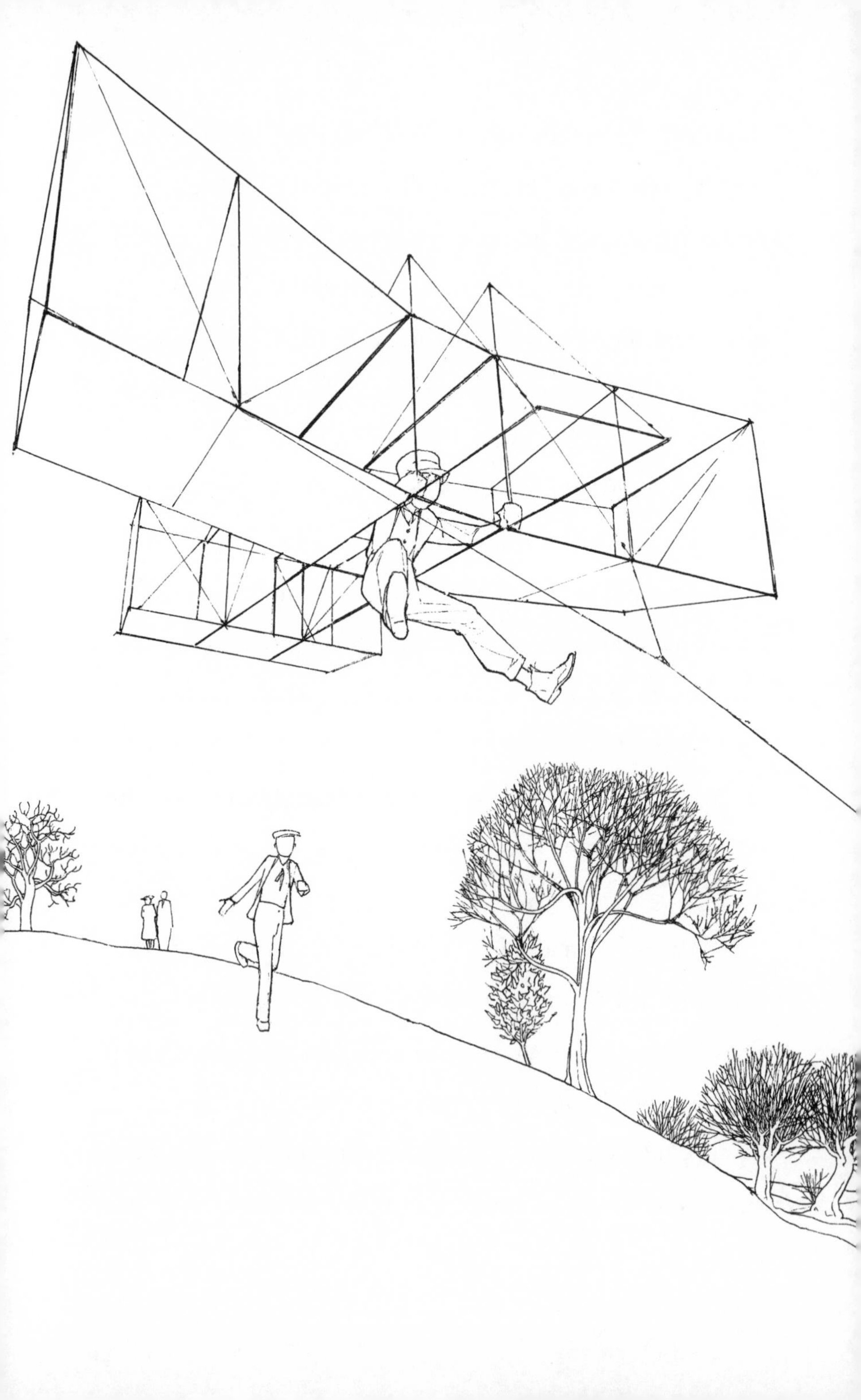

Papa asked them to wait for him. He had an important letter to write and send before he could meet them.

It was cloudy, and wind blew silver ripples on the lake. "I hope it doesn't get too windy to fly," Willy said, and the wind blew a gust in defiance.

"It might even rain. Then we're sunk for sure. Why don't you go ahead now," Guy said, "before the weather gets worse."

Willy took the pilot's position, and Guy helped him support the glider.

Sarah stood at the bottom of the slope near the lake. "Aren't you going to wait for Papa?" she called.

"Willy's ready to go," said Guy.

Willy hooked his arms over the side bars and shouted, "I like a challenge." He broke into a run toward the edge and was airborne instantly in a gust of wind. The wind lifted the glider four feet into the air. It rose straight up above them instead of gliding toward the lake. The wind carried it along the slope. It blew with such sudden force that it twisted a wing, and like a bird with a broken wing, the glider, with Willy clinging to it, lunged straight down toward the beach.

Sarah screamed. Guy watched, holding his breath.

Willy lost his grip and slipped from the glider. He reached out to break his fall, then hit the ground and rolled onto his side. The glider hopped along the shore, then bounced into the shallow water while Guy and Sarah rushed to Willy.

Willy clutched his left wrist. His face was white and his eyes glowed with pain. "I think it's broken," he said. Then he threw up.

Guy and Sarah helped Willy back to the hotel. They ran into Papa, who spared them a scolding and hurried off to fetch a doctor. The doctor agreed with Willy: his wrist was broken. After the doctor treated Willy, Guy and Papa went back to retrieve the waterlogged glider from the lake.

"I should have waited for you," Guy said.

"You should have done," said Papa, "but it was an accident. It might have happened even if I had been there."

They took the glider apart, but saved the pieces and strips of sheets and pillowcases. Sarah helped.

"Are you going to try again?" she asked.

"Maybe," Guy said, "but probably not this summer."

With his wrist wrapped in a cast for the rest of vacation, Willy couldn't hang from gliders anymore. He couldn't practice piano or flute anymore either, not until his cast came off.

Guy and Sarah went to tell Willy's parents that they were sorry about what happened. His father was calm and understanding. Frau Schiller was sitting on a green brocade chair. Her face was as pale as Willy's had been when he broke his wrist. Guy could feel her bright black eyes fixed on him as she spoke. "I know how sorry you are about Willy's injury. We are upset too." Guy was surprised by what she said next. "But you know, we have to accept the bad things that happen to us. Perhaps we can learn from them." She shook her head gently as if she hadn't quite convinced herself. "I don't believe I've told you that I had been hoping–well, there was no definite invitation, but I was hoping that Willy could play for the emperor. He arrives here at the end of the month."

Willy stood beside his mother, but far enough behind her that she couldn't see his lips turn upward in an impish smile and his eyes crinkle shut. Willy wasn't disappointed at all.

All the way back to the hotel Sarah kept chattering about the emperor. "Who is this emperor, anyway? Is he like a king? What does an emperor do? Will we get to meet him?"

"His name is Franz Josef I, and he is the ruler of the Austrian Empire. I guess he's like a king, but instead of a kingdom, he has an empire. And I don't expect we'll meet him. We haven't had emperors in France since Napoléon," Guy pointed out. "We're a republic. We vote for a president."

"If we do go to see the emperor, then Maman and Papa won't know how to behave. I'll have to ask Willy."

Although Guy's parents were planning on departing August thirtieth, they decided to stay when they found out the Austrian emperor was coming that day.

Sarah asked Willy, "How will he notice me in a big crowd?" and Willy told her to hold up a bouquet of flowers.

"I don't see how anyone could miss you, Sarah, with your curly red hair and freckles," Guy teased.

A band played before the train station and the crowd grew as people waited for the emperor's train to arrive.

The mayor stood with a group of city leaders, pulling out his watch every once in a while. Then the train whistle blew and the band stopped. Sarah, Guy, and Willy wiggled their way to a clearing where they could see the platform on which the mayor stood.

The crowd pressed forward as the train stopped. Soldiers in blue uniforms strutted onto the platform, then made way for a small, thin man, standing very stiff, in a blue uniform laden with medals. The mayor bowed before the man with a shiny bald head and fluffy mustaches that hid half of his face.

The crowd waved and shouted greetings, and the band began to play. Willy cheered and Sarah tossed flowers in the direction of Franz Josef I. Guy was disappointed. He had expected the emperor to be taller and younger and somehow grander. Instead he was just an old man in a uniform. But Guy didn't tell Willy or Sarah what he thought.

7

GROWING APART: SUMMER 1910

During the winter rain fell every day, not only in Paris but in the regions around the city. Day after day after day the rain tumbled down onto the rooftops and streets and into the Seine River that flows through the center of the city. The river rose higher and higher. When Papa told them that the water was up to the soldier's neck on the Alma Bridge, Guy and Sarah and Maman had to go see it. They stood on the right bank of the river and stared at the bridge pile with the soldier statue on it. Usually the water was at his feet, but now the muddy, churning river swept around the bridge columns and up to the soldier's chin.

"The Seine has overflowed its banks and submerged the quais and now it runs through the streets of Paris," Guy wrote to Willy. "There's never been anything like it."

"We are fortunate to live on higher ground," Papa told the family. "The water will never reach us at the Place d'Iéna. But our fellow citizens are threatened."

Hundreds of Parisians, young and old, businessmen and soldiers and workers, piled up sandbags all over the city. They built wooden terraces so that people could get from place to place. Papa took Guy to help fight the flood. Maman and Sarah collected clothes and blankets and supplies for those who had lost everything.

"It's exciting," Guy wrote Willy. "Everyone is so focused. Everyone works together. Papa said it is the first time he can remember seeing all of the people joined in a single cause."

When the river flowed through the printer's offices and flooded the warehouse and equipment, Maman was afraid they would be ruined.

"The flood will end. The warehouse will have to be cleaned up. That's all. Then everyone will go back to work," Papa said calmly.

Finally the flood did end. The waters receded, leaving a slimy layer of mud over the cobblestone streets. Buildings and shops and apartments that had been flooded were cold and damp. Everywhere a strong odor of dead fish and mildew filled the air.

After the disaster had ended, Maman suggested one evening, "Perhaps we should not go on vacation this year. We could go to your mother's house, Edouard. It's been shut up for years, but we could open it again. A trip to Normandy wouldn't be expensive at all."

"Maman," Sarah complained.

"Must we?" Guy sounded hurt.

"I won't hear of it," Papa said. "We'll travel to Lake Constance as usual. Business has its ups and downs, and last year being particularly good, I say we take our usual vacation."

Off they went in August and arrived in Bregenz a few weeks after Willy and his parents. Willy's mother had taken a turn for the worse that summer. She spent most of her time inside, resting. She asked Willy to play for her almost every afternoon. Only after she fell asleep was he able to join the others. Willy invited Guy and Sarah to come listen so at least they could be together. For a while Guy would listen to the music, but then he would look out the window and think how he would rather be out there doing something than sitting and listening to music, even if his best friend was playing it.

Many afternoons Guy took off on his own while Sarah went to Willy's. He followed his own trails into the forest and climbed hills and rocky cliffs. He took his sketch-book and drew trees, flowers, birds, and the lake. He drew pictures of the village below. Then he turned to sketching people in the village. Young men with sun-burned faces and strong arms, girls and women who went barefoot and threaded ribbons in their braids. He wanted to know more about these people and their lives away from the tourists and the big hotels.

Then he met Amalie, who lived on a farm. She came to the village to sell eggs and butter. Guy sketched her with her long black braids and green eyes and gave the picture to her. Smiling, she took the picture, and the next day she gave him a garland of clover.

Willy teased him when he saw the garland around Guy's neck. "So that's what you've been doing these afternoons, weaving garlands of clover."

"Not exactly," Guy said. "I'm studying people. Come with me tomorrow."

"I don't know if I can leave Mutti. Maybe later in the afternoon."

"Ask Sarah to keep her company. Sarah will do anything for you."

Willy went to the village with Guy the next day. Amalie was there, and with her was another girl, her cousin Marta. She was small with amber eyes and brown hair.

Willy agreed with Guy that studying people could be interesting. Every chance he had, he slipped out with Guy. "Mutti loves to hear you read in French," Willy told Sarah, and thanked her for spending so much time with his mother.

Sarah complained that when she wanted to play, she couldn't find them. "Why don't you want to swim anymore? Or sail your boats? You haven't sailed your boats in two years."

"We're too old for children's games. We have other things to do," Guy told her.

Later, on the way to the village, Willy said, "You were too cross with Sarah."

"I didn't mean to be," Guy said. "She'd spoil everything. She's much younger than us, younger than Amalie and Marta too. She wouldn't fit in, especially not today. Remember our plans. Are you feeling strong, Willy?"

"I'm always strong." Willy held up his bony arm and flexed his muscle. Then he punched at Guy, who ducked and escaped the blow.

Striking at each other and dodging, they made their way to meet Amalie and Marta. They were laughing loudly and didn't see the girls waiting for them by the church.

"Are you fighting over me?" Amalie said.

"Or me?" Marta teased. She held a basket of food.

"No, we're fighting over who gets to row first," Guy said.

Amalie had borrowed her uncle's boat, and they were going to row across the cove to picnic on the opposite shore.

"It's me," Willy shouted. "I'll go first."

They left the village and followed a cow path through

the meadow to a dock by the water's edge. Guy got into the rowboat tied to the dock and settled into the rowing position. Willy helped Marta and Amalie into the boat, untied the rope, pushed off, and stepped into the stern.

"Wait!" Guy shouted. "There's only one oar."

Amalie cried out. "That can't be. I rowed over with two oars."

Marta started laughing. "We'll go in circles with only one oar."

"It's not funny," Guy said. He looked to Willy for support.

But Willy was laughing, too. He threw his head back and his eyes were nearly closed.

"You don't have to go in circles!" Sarah's voice called over their laughter. She stood on the dock. She held the oar upright in both hands like a lance. "If you will let me go with you, I'll give you the oar."

"Good heavens, Sarah! What are you doing here?"

"I followed you."

"Followed us? How long have you been doing that?" Willy asked.

"Only once or twice, but it's long enough to know where you go every day."

"No fair," Guy muttered, uncomfortable, mad, embarrassed that Sarah had been spying on them.

"All's fair in love and war," Sarah shouted back.

"What nonsense!" Guy said. "Talk to her, Willy. You can persuade her to give us the oar."

"Who is that girl?" Amalie said.

"If you want to know who I am, ask Willy," Sarah said angrily. "I guess he forgot to tell you all about me."

Amalie and Marta turned to Willy.

"She's just Guy's little sister," he said, shrugging.

Sarah let the oar drop. Everyone watched it strike the dock, then roll into the lake with a splash. A bigger splash followed. Sarah had jumped off the dock into the lake.

Was she trying to get the oar? Was she mad? Regardless of what she intended to do, she had gotten their attention by jumping in the lake. Guy felt uneasy as he watched the bubbles on the surface. Sarah was a good swimmer. Why hadn't she come up yet? Were her clothes weighing her down? Her hat drifted away on the surface. Suddenly her head popped up through the bubbles. She gulped in air. She treaded water to keep her head up.

Guy moved swiftly to the back of the rowboat. Amalie and Marta shifted to the middle, and Willy, ghostlike, stayed in the front. Guy paddled first on one side, then the other. Willy leaned forward and grabbed the oar from the lake. He held it out as the boat glided toward Sarah.

"Take the oar, Sarah," Willy said, "and hold on."

Sarah clung to the oar and Willy pulled her close to the boat. Guy paddled to the dock, and Willy with the help of the others pulled Sarah from the lake.

"We'll have to take you home now so you can change," Guy said.

"I can't go home all dripping wet," Sarah said.

"Come back to our cottage, Sarah. You can wear my other dress while yours dries out," Amalie said.

Guy was more relieved than angry, even if Sarah had spoiled their picnic.

"Guy, you didn't tell me you had a little sister," Marta said.

"There are lots of things Guy didn't tell you," Sarah said. She stared at Guy with narrowed eyes. "And lots of things he didn't tell *me*, either."

Sarah didn't follow them again that summer. Guy tried to make it up to her. He unpacked *Zéphyr* and let her sail his toy boat whenever she wished. But if Sarah had asked to go to the village with them, Guy would have told her no. Sarah never asked, though.

Willy wondered why Sarah was acting strange, why she didn't laugh or even tease him the way she used to. When Guy asked Sarah why she was ignoring Willy, she said that she would never laugh again. Willy had broken her heart.

8

MISSING WILLY: 1911-1912

Back in Paris that fall, Guy wrote letters to Willy, as always, and also wrote to Amalie. Willy answered all of Guy's letters, but Amalie answered none. This was not surprising. Amalie and Marta couldn't write. Nor could they read. Amalie would probably have to take her letters to the village priest so that he could read them to her. Guy didn't like the idea of the priest reading his letters to Amalie. After a while, it became harder and harder to think of what to say to Amalie. Finally he stopped writing.

Willy mentioned Sarah in a letter Guy received in February. "I miss you, Guy. And Sarah too."

When Guy told Sarah, she immediately wrote a letter to Willy. Guy asked her what she had said, but it was private. "Between Willy and me," she said. Willy answered her letter, but again Sarah said, "Between Willy and me."

After that, Willy stopped writing. Studies, perhaps, Guy thought, or constant piano practice probably kept him from answering Guy's letters. Still, it was strange. In fact, it was the first time Willy had not written for such a long time. What bothered Guy most was that several times he had written to invite Willy to come home with them at the end of summer vacation. He had asked Maman and Papa about it, and they agreed that it would be a good time for Willy to come. Why hadn't Willy written back? Why wasn't he as excited as Guy?

Plans went ahead for vacation, and they left on July twenty-seventh, earlier than usual. Guy was certain that Willy would already be there, and he was surprised that Willy didn't come to meet them. There was no message waiting for them from Willy or his parents to explain why they hadn't arrived yet.

After they had settled in, Guy and Sarah went to Willy's hotel. The receptionist told them, "No, we're expecting the Schillers, but they haven't arrived yet."

Guy felt lost as he and Sarah went through the motions of vacation. When Guy walked along the lakeshore, he would look over his shoulder expecting to see Willy run up to him.

Sarah would follow his gaze and say sadly, "I wonder why Willy's not here yet."

Three days passed, then four, and still Willy didn't appear.

"You'll come, of course." Papa had bought tickets for a steamship excursion across the lake to visit some beautiful gardens on an island.

"I'd rather stay here. In case Willy comes."

"We'll only be gone for a day, back later in the afternoon. If Willy comes, he'll see you soon enough."

As they crossed the lake and strolled through gardens on Mainau Island, all that Guy could think was how much he wished Willy were with them. He thought about Willy's mother too. The sight of all of these beautiful flowers would surely cheer her up.

When they returned to the hotel, it was evening. They were tired from the sun and fresh air and the wind. The hotel clerk handed Guy's father a small white envelope bordered in black. The letter was from Willy's father. Willy's mother had died. They would not be coming this summer.

"What sad news," Maman said.

"She was not well." Papa's voice was soft and low. "Tuberculosis."

Sarah began to cry and Guy put his arm around her. He thought about Willy's mother. Last summer she had remained inside, lying down most of the time. She had always wanted Willy nearby. Guy wondered if she could have known that was her last summer on earth. Was it possible to know?

"Vati is miserable," Willy wrote in a letter that came the following week. "He sits and stares and says nothing all day. All I want is for things to be the way they were. Like last summer. And then I remember how I kept sneaking out, you know, to meet Marta and Amalie, and all Mutti wanted was for me to be with her, near her. Sarah was the one who kept her company. Please tell Sarah how grateful I am. I think about you both."

"Why did she have to die?" Sarah said when Guy read her Willy's letter. Her eyes were red from crying. "Poor Willy. How sad he must be. I don't know what I would do if Maman died. It would be horrible. I would never be happy again."

Guy noticed a change in Sarah. She tried hard to

please Maman. She didn't even protest having her hair braided tightly or having to wear the blue-ribboned hat that she hated. Guy spent more time with his parents too. The restlessness he usually felt, the urge to be somewhere else, to be doing something, had left him. Like a sailboat on a windless day, he didn't drift far from home and was content to sit in folding chairs on the beach and converse in soft tones with his parents. For the first time he could remember, he looked forward to returning to Paris.

Their lives went on just as before once they were back in Paris. Guy worried about Willy, though, especially since his friend didn't write often. Then in the spring a letter came from Willy saying he would spend the summer near Prague, with his aunt and uncle and two cousins. His father would join him later. His aunt Petra was his mother's sister, and his uncle was a music professor, so Willy's visit probably had another purpose.

When Guy read the letter to Sarah, she ran from him, crying.

When it came time for Papa to buy their train tickets for holiday, Maman said, "Perhaps we should go somewhere else this summer."

They went to Brittany and stayed at a hotel in La Baule. All day they spent on the beach. In the evening they ate delicious seafood: shrimp, crabs, mussels, and scallops. Maman and Papa ate raw oysters too; Sarah tried them, but Guy couldn't bring himself to swallow the slimy seafood.

Guy walked for hours alone on the beach. He stared at the waves. He couldn't look away from the white curls as they splashed onto the sand. He painted the waves again and again. In his paintings he could hold them in the air and stop them from crashing to the beach beneath them. In his paintings he could stop time. If only he had such power in real life, he would have used it two summers ago.

9

THE ONLY PEOPLE IN THE WORLD: SUMMER 1913

When they learned that Willy and his father would return to Bregenz the next summer, there was no question that Guy and his family would be there too.

On the train ride to Lake Constance, Guy was quiet. Sarah wanted to chat and kept getting up and down, too excited to remain seated. But Guy read and sketched and let his mind wander. He kept thinking about Willy. They hadn't been together for two summers. In that time they had written few letters. Schoolwork took up Guy's time. He had begun to prepare for the difficult exams he would take, the written exam at the end of his last term next year and the oral exam in the fall. Once he had his baccalaureate degree, perhaps Papa would agree that he could study at the School of Fine Arts instead of law or philosophy at the university.

All he knew about Willy's life now was that he had begun classes at the music conservatory. Guy told himself that Willy must have been so involved in his music that he hadn't had time to write. A thought kept nagging him on the trip: Were they still best friends? Or had things changed in these two years?

Finally Sarah persuaded Guy to walk the length of the train. "Like we always used to do, Guy."

When the train reached the Alps, the sight of the gigantic mountains cheered Guy. Even the tunnels reminded him of happy summers. As they got closer to Lake Constance, Guy got up and began to walk back and forth, staring out the windows.

Maman opened the compartment door and scolded him gently, as if he were a child. "Guy, please, come sit down. First Sarah, and now you, disturbing the other passengers—pacing up and down like that."

Guy sat down with a sigh beside Sarah, but by now they both fidgeted restlessly.

The train slowed as it entered the village. A huge crowd of people filled the platform. The streets were overrun with men and women and children too.

"What is going on?" Maman asked.

"It must be some sort of celebration," Papa said.

"What celebration?" Sarah wondered aloud.

They made their way slowly through the mass of people. They didn't look like the usual group of vacationers. Guy heard French, German, Italian, English, and several other languages he didn't recognize.

"You're lucky to have found a cottage," the coachman told them. He drove them away from the village to a group of cottages in a clearing near the woods. "No room in any hotels in town. There are thousands here today for a big meeting. They're all talking about peace."

"Oh dear," Maman said. "People usually talk about peace when they are worried about war."

"But France isn't at war with anyone now, is it?" Sarah asked.

"France hasn't fought a war in Europe since 1870," Papa said. "I was four then, and my mother took me to live in our house in Normandy. We left just in time, she said. My father had to stay in Paris, though, and he told us stories about the siege, how the Prussian army surrounded the city and the people had nothing to eat."

"That was a long time ago," said Sarah. "We always have plenty to eat now."

"Just because France isn't at war doesn't mean people aren't fighting. Look at the war in the Balkans," Guy said.

"They will always be fighting in the Balkans," Papa said.

"Then maybe they do need to talk about peace," Sarah said as they arrived at their cottage.

It was actually a farmhouse with four rooms downstairs and two upstairs under the slanted roof. It belonged to a farmer who lived nearby.

Their first guests of the summer were Willy and his father. Willy had grown much taller. He was almost as tall as Guy, and thinner. He had a thin black mustache and looked older than seventeen. Seeing Willy's mustache, Guy decided that he would grow one this summer.

Maman and Papa greeted Willy and Herr Schiller. They did mention how sorry they were about Frau Schiller's death, but they didn't dwell on it. Instead, they talked about their trip and the beautiful weather and asked how Willy's studies were going. The conversation went on and on. Willy listened politely, hardly saying anything. He smiled whenever he looked at Guy and Sarah, but his smile looked different–maybe because of his mustache–and his eyes looked sad. He was probably remembering past vacations, Guy thought, and missing his mother. Or maybe Willy had changed.

After tea, Willy excused himself. "Would anyone care to join me in a walk along the lake?"

Guy and Sarah jumped up and hurried out the door ahead of Willy. Then they turned to excuse themselves from their parents, who remained to talk. Willy walked between Guy and Sarah in silence until they reached the lake. Willy began to run, then Guy chased after him, and Sarah shouted, "Wait! Wait! I'm coming too."

They raced along the shore like colts in spring. Guy caught up with Willy, and they ran side by side along the beach until they were out of breath. Then they collapsed on the sand. A few moments later, Sarah flopped down beside them.

Willy stared out at the lake. "From this point the lake is at its longest."

"So long that you can see the curve of the earth," Guy added.

When Sarah got her breath back, she shouted, "I see! I see them–lots of curves of the earth."

Guy and Willy burst into laugher. When they finally

stopped, Sarah said, "Promise me that we'll be together all this summer."

They joined hands and raised them to the sky. "Nothing can separate us," they vowed in unison.

Sarah ran errands with Maman one morning. When she returned, she flashed one of her I-know-something-that-you-don't-know looks. Guy could feel her need to tell. He didn't have to wait long.

"Amalie has married a farmer and Marta has gone to work as a maid in Salzburg," she announced. "That's what the man at the dairy told me."

"I didn't know you were so interested in ancient history," Willy joked.

"It's not so long ago," Sarah said. "I thought you might like to know."

"Not as much as you do," Guy said. "I had forgotten about them. That was a long time ago. You were just a little girl then."

"A good swimmer though," Willy said.

"And good at spying too," Guy said.

Sarah waved her hands. "All right, you win." And Sarah said no more about the two village girls.

But the rest of the day Guy found himself thinking

about Amalie. That summer three years ago he had even wondered what it would be like to marry her and live in a cottage and go barefoot. But not anymore. Willy is right, Guy thought, ancient history.

One afternoon Willy played a recital for Guy and Sarah alone. "I want to show you some of the things I've been doing."

As he listened, Guy thought, *There is something different about Willy. He is so confident, so sure of himself, of what he wants to do in life.* Guy felt just a bit jealous.

When Willy stopped, both Guy and Sarah applauded.

"Beautiful," said Sarah.

"You will be famous someday," Guy said.

"Do you like the first three pieces?"

"Very much," said Sarah.

"Better than Chopin." Guy had recognized the composer of the nocturne Willy played last.

"I wrote them myself," Willy said. "I don't want to just play other people's music, no matter how grand. You cannot imagine how sick I am of waltzes. Anyway, the world is changing. Can't you feel it? Music is changing. I want to be part of it, to do something new too."

"I think it's time for you to come to Paris, Willy." Guy

was thinking that Willy would have come much sooner if his mother hadn't died. "Paris will be new and different for you. There is music everywhere," said Guy. "You'll stay with us and you can study at the conservatory or wherever you wish. And I promise, you won't have to travel in a trunk."

Papa and Maman liked the idea of a visit from Willy, but they were firm that it would have to be next summer. "You have your exams to prepare for, Guy, at the end of your final term. But I don't see why Willy can't return with us next summer."

"I'll have something besides exams to look forward to," Guy told Willy. "I am so tired of stuffy books, lectures, exams–it's not real life. I sometimes wonder how I can ever be a great painter if I don't experience real life, not just what I read about in books."

"What do you mean?" Willy asked.

"I can't explain, exactly. I'm restless, I suppose. I want to see other places and people. And I want to test myself in some way."

"Don't you test yourself each time you paint a picture?"

"No, I don't think I do. Not yet. I always seem to paint what makes me happy or what I think is beautiful."

"What else is there?" Willy said.

"You philosophers can ramble on, but I know what I'm going to do. I'm going to England," said Sarah. "I'm going to be an English poet."

"Sarah is in love with Keats and Shelley," Guy explained.

"And Shakespeare," said Sarah. "Maybe I should become an actress instead."

"Ah," said Willy, "like your namesake, Sarah Bernhardt."

Guy shook his head. "I think Maman would be displeased if you made a career in the theater," he said. "How can you marry a respectable gentleman if you become an actress?"

"But you are already engaged," Willy said, "to a very respectable gentleman. Remember?" He made a deep bow.

Sarah blushed crimson.

On the day before they had to leave, they picnicked in a mountain meadow. Sarah made up songs and sang while Willy played the flute to accompany her. Guy sketched the mountain and the trees. Then he made a sketch of them all: three happy friends in summer light.

He called it "The Only People in the World" and gave it to Willy.

Too soon it was time to say good-bye.

"Au revoir. Auf wiedersehen," Guy called to Willy from the train.

Then Sarah shouted in English, "Parting is such sweet sorrow."

"Bis sommer. A l'été prochain." Willy waved at them, smiling with his eyes crinkled shut.

Guy and Sarah watched until the train rounded a curve and Willy disappeared from sight, then Guy whispered to Sarah, "Until next summer."

10

WHAT DOES THAT HAVE TO DO WITH US?

SUMMER 1914

Before he could enjoy the pleasure of summer vacation, Guy had to endure the long hours of study during the fall and winter, and the pain of an examination in June.

Guy sat at a desk in the examination hall with his classmates, nervous young men all hoping to pass this difficult exam. An instructor passed out the test booklets and pencils to each student.

Even before Guy looked at the questions, he felt his hands go cold. His stomach began to churn. Then he looked at the first question and his mind went blank. He couldn't remember who Montaigne was, let alone what his philosophy of tolerance was. How could Guy write about something he couldn't remember?

He gripped his pencil, scanning his memory, and wrote the number "1" on his page. He waited for a thought, any thought, to enter his mind. He drew a circle around the number, he chewed his pencil, then he looked up at the clock on the wall. For months he had read, studied, and practiced writing essay after essay. He couldn't fail now. Maman and Papa would be so disappointed.

He took a deep breath. Maybe the other questions would be easier. He searched through the booklet, reading questions about Latin, literature, history, and Greek. Not subjects he liked to think about. Why couldn't the exam have questions about images and color and light? But there were none. Finally he read a question about the art of the Renaissance. At last a question he could answer.

Once he began writing, his stomach stopped churning, and his mind began to fill with facts he had read, theories he had studied. Details and facts poured into his mind, and he couldn't write fast enough to capture them all.

Guy passed his exam, but he was far from the top in his scores.

"You contemplated before leaping in and writing whatever came to your mind, didn't you?" Papa asked, making a question out of what he had told Guy before the exam.

"But of course," Guy said.

"We are pleased that you succeeded," Maman said.

"With your permission, I would like to enroll in the School of Fine Arts."

"But, Guy." Papa sighed and shook his head.

"Perhaps he should do painting," Maman said. "He's very good at that."

"Not very practical," Papa said.

"But it does make sense, Papa. I can begin at the School of Fine Arts, if they'll have me. In two years I'll be called up for military service anyway. And then I'll be in the army for three years—"

"Two years," Maman interrupted. "The newly elected government has promised to reduce the term from three to two years."

"Maybe," said Papa, "but nothing is sure until it happens."

"Then one thing is sure," Guy said, smiling. "I've passed my exam."

The argument ended for now. Guy didn't bring the

subject up again, but he began his application to the art school. He also continued his impractical habit of painting.

Sarah began to count the days until they would leave for vacation. "Forty-two days till August first," she would tell the family. "Forty-one days, forty days . . . "

At dinner one evening Sarah sat down and announced with a smile, "Eighteen days."

Guy smiled back, but her cheerfulness didn't have an effect on Papa, who looked gloomy despite the fact that tomorrow was Bastille Day, a national holiday. "I am very sorry . . . " he murmured. Then he spoke louder. "I am very sorry to tell you, we may have to cancel our plans to go to Austria in August."

"Papa! You can't mean it!" Sarah shouted.

Papa's words struck Guy like a blow. Speechless, he stared at Papa, waiting for an explanation.

"I'm afraid that a war may begin, a war between Austria and Serbia. Leaders are always rattling their sabers and talking of war, but this time I'm afraid it may be serious."

"Our new prime minister won't be rattling sabers, Edouard," Maman said. "You've said as much yourself since the Socialists were elected. They are very much against war."

Papa listened to Maman with the same sad look on his face. "I don't know if our leaders can do anything about it. It's because of the assassination. The Austrian archduke and his wife were shot in Sarajevo."

Guy remembered reading the headlines about it, a front-page story over two weeks ago. A student had shot them both, but other men had been involved in the plot. "But they caught him, didn't they? The man who shot them, and the others involved in the plot too?"

"I know that was terrible," Sarah said. "But I don't see what the archduke has to do with us."

Papa explained. "The men who plotted were all Serbian. Austria wants to punish Serbia."

"Couldn't they just punish the murderers?"

"No doubt they will, but I don't know if that will satisfy the Austrians."

Why would it be so hard to satisfy the Austrians? Guy thought about Willy and his parents and the people he saw every summer in Austria. Why would they want to punish people who didn't do anything wrong? The Austrians were reasonable people.

"Even if Austria does go to war, I don't see why France should get involved," Guy said.

"France may have no choice. The Russians are allies of the Serbs. And we are allies of the Russians. From what I understand, if Austria attacks Serbia, then the czar of Russia will defend Serbia with his army. If that happens, France will side with Russia and fight Austria too."

"France at war with Austria?" Guy went cold as he realized what Papa meant.

He turned to Sarah to see if she understood that Willy's country might be at war with France.

"This is too confusing," Sarah said. "It's silly. Why should the Russian czar spoil our plans for holiday?"

"Sarah." Papa's voice was gentle. He shook his head. "There are things in the world much, much bigger than all of us."

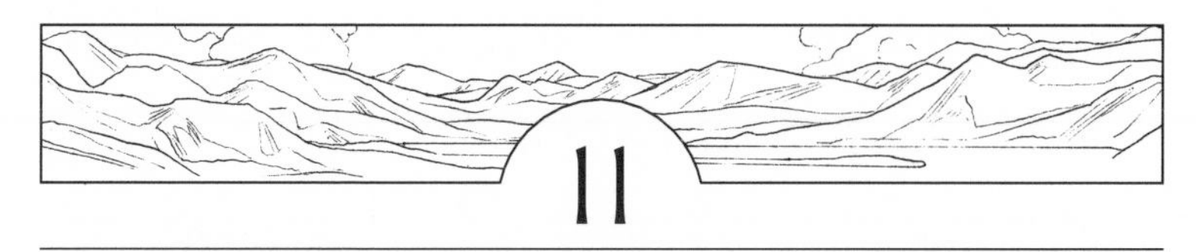

11

TALK OF NOTHING ELSE: 1914

Everything happened quickly after July 28, when Austria and Hungary declared war on Serbia. The next day Russia called for its army to mobilize. Then Germany, an ally of Austria, declared war on Russia on August 1. Just as Papa had predicted, France could not avoid going to war. All the newspapers that Saturday, August 1, announced the mobilization of the French army. Then on August 3, Germany declared war on France.

Guy and his parents would not be leaving Paris for a holiday on the shores of Lake Constance. Enemies weren't supposed to spend vacation together.

Guy was surprised to receive a letter from Willy after

France had declared war on Austria on August 11. He thought the borders would be closed, and no mail would be delivered. Maybe the postman hadn't noticed Willy's address on the envelope. Otherwise he might have thrown the letter away. Already angry Parisians had wrecked a German butcher's shop and two Austrian bakeries.

Willy's letter was dated July 27, and Guy was sure it would be the last one until the war ended.

"In Vienna people are talking about going to war," Willy wrote. "Yesterday the army mobilized, and now many think it is only a matter of days. If war begins, Vati will be called to join his reserve brigade. If it lasts long enough, I too will be called, or I may enlist. Me, a soldier? Can you believe it?

"Everything is happening so fast. The ground is shifting beneath our feet. What will you do, Guy? Of course, there is no question of going on holiday. I am sorry to miss seeing you and Sarah, but we have no choice. Write soon if you can. Your friend, Willy."

It was too late to write back.

Guy wondered if Vienna was the same as Paris. Every day he saw soldiers marching through the streets.

At the station women gathered to give the men in uniform flowers and kiss them good-bye. Already the twenty-year-olds had been called up, and soon the nineteen-year-olds would be called, that is, if they didn't enlist right away.

Everywhere in the neighborhood people were talking about the war. Shopkeepers chatted about the brave soldiers and how they would show the Germans, the *Boche* they called them, after a word that meant beer.

"A little charge here, another there, and the Boche will be running back home," Guy heard the postman shout one day. "We citizens must defend our country," the baker told Maman, and the next day a sign in his window read "Closed. The owner has gone to war."

The people of Paris were all focused on the same thing. The excitement reminded Guy of the way people acted during the flood. But now it was not just Paris but all of France that was focused on one subject: defeating the enemy.

At home they talked about the war too, at every meal.

"Will it be over soon?" Maman asked Papa. "Monsieur Pasquier, the cobbler, has two sons in the army. He said he expects them back for Christmas."

"He may be right. Who is to know? If we show the Germans our strength, they won't press us," Papa said. "But you know that if it lasts longer, I will try again to volunteer."

"Edouard, with your heart condition, they will tell you to go home again—as they should." Maman turned to Guy. "I do hope it is over soon. Then, Guy, you won't have to think about being a soldier during wartime."

"You worry too much, Maman," Guy said. Although he thought every day about signing up, he kept his thoughts to himself.

Guy tried to prepare for the second part of his exam, when he would have to stand before a group of professors in the fall and answer their questions. He couldn't concentrate on studying. He found it hard to spend hours painting anymore. Every day brought a new story of bravery to the neighborhood. Monsieur Blanchard had fought courageously at Charleroi. Monsieur Beyle, the chemist, had been wounded at a battle at Neufchâteau. He came home with his arm in a sling and said that as soon as he was well, he would return to the front.

They read in the morning newspapers thrilling accounts of battle and hand-to-hand combat in which the French were successful against the Germans. They read of horrible acts of murder of civilians committed by the Germans.

"I don't understand it," said Sarah. "How could the Austrians be friends of such terrible people? We have been to Austria and they seem to be decent, civilized people. Like Willy."

"Still, Sarah, decent, civilized people manage to get involved in wars," Papa said.

"They should fight by the rules," Guy said. "If not, they should be punished."

"When the war is over, they will be punished," Maman said. "And everyone says it will be over soon."

"I hope so, dear," said Papa, "but whenever it ends, France must win this war."

They all agreed with Papa.

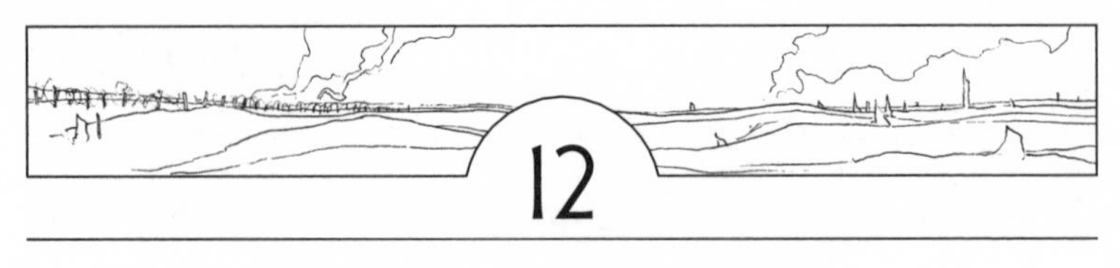

12

BOMBS OVER PARIS: SEPTEMBER 1914

At the end of August, Guy took his portfolio to the School of Fine Arts. Because he had so much to carry, Maman suggested he take a cab. "If you can find one," she said.

Guy ended up in one of the old horse-drawn cabs that had been dusted out and put back on the streets now that many taxicabs were being used by the military. There were so few automobiles on the streets that Guy wondered if all of the cars had been called up for duty like the soldiers. The clip-clop of the horse's hooves on the cobblestones made Guy feel as if he had gone back in time. So did the Fine Arts building, an ugly blocklike building, dark and gloomy within. He introduced himself to the director's assistant, Monsieur Bresson, who apologized that so many classes had to be canceled.

"It's the war, of course," he said, waving his hands in the air and shaking his head. "Professors have gone. Students have gone. I don't know what we'll do."

Guy did meet one student, an American who spoke excellent French and told him he would be going to work for the American Embassy soon. He didn't see why he should be painting all day when he could be of use. "The U.S. is neutral, officially," the young man said, "but I can tell you that I personally am hoping for a French victory."

Guy watched a man painting a still life of two lemons and a pitcher arranged on a table before him. He was French and very old. He looked as if he might be a hundred. As he daubed a speck of yellow paint on the lemon he had outlined, Guy thought it would probably take him another hundred years to paint the second lemon.

Again Monsieur Bresson waved his hands as he spoke. "I'm afraid we can no longer offer models for life drawing. The men have joined the army, and the young women are looking for work in the factories. But everything will be back to normal once the war is over."

Guy left his portfolio with Monsieur Bresson, who

promised that the director would look at it shortly. With nothing heavy to carry, Guy decided to walk home. He strolled along the quai beside the river, thinking about the old artist and the young American he had just met. Could he shut himself in a room and paint pictures of lemons while a war was going on? He looked up and saw the tip of the Eiffel Tower ahead of him. He thought of Grand-maman and how much she had disliked the tower. "Ugly and useless," she had said.

What would she say if she were alive now and learned how useful the tower had become in wartime? Now the army used it as an observation and communications post. Vital messages traveled to and from the tower every day. And near the top, guns had been installed to defend the city.

Guy came to the Iéna Bridge and turned to go up away from the river toward their apartment, on the other side of Place Iéna. It was nearly six o'clock and he began to hurry. Then he heard an airplane engine and stopped to scan the sky. A few passersby stopped to look up. A man pointed to the sky way across town.

"It's a German aviator!" the man cried out just as Guy saw the speck in the sky. It grew larger and then hovered

above the city like a graceful bird.

An enemy airplane, flying freely over Paris? Guy couldn't believe that no French guns had shot it down yet. Where were the French pilots? Guy watched anxiously, waiting for a French airplane to appear.

A dark cylinder fell from the aircraft. Then Guy could see a plume of black smoke rising from a rooftop. Then two more bombs fell, and the pilot flew away unchallenged.

Guy rushed from the chattering crowd.

"Where have you been, Guy? We were so worried. Didn't you hear the explosion just now?" Sarah said when he entered the apartment.

"Sarah, I've just seen the most incredible thing." Guy described the German airplane that had flown over Paris. Enemy or not, the pilot had shown skill and courage to fly all the way to Paris alone like that.

The evening papers were full of the story. An elderly woman had been killed when a bomb fell on her apartment. But no one else had been hurt. The pilot had even dropped a flyer that said: "The German army is at the gates of Paris. Nothing remains for you but to surrender. –Lieutenant von Heidssen."

"What does he mean?" Maman asked. "How could the Germans be so near in such a short time? We haven't been at war for a month."

"I can't understand it myself," Papa said. "There has been nothing in the papers or the dispatches until this German pilot shows up. To be honest, I don't think the papers would tell the public all of the details for fear of a panic. Can you imagine what would happen if they announced that the Germans were at the gates?"

"Everyone would want to leave," Guy said.

"In fact," Papa turned to Mama, "perhaps you and Sarah should leave the city. Maybe it's still possible to go to Normandy and stay in the old house there."

Mama shook her head. "I won't leave you here."

"Me either," said Sarah.

"Maybe the pilot is just saying that to frighten us," Guy said.

"Nonetheless, if there is a siege of Paris, we will be in a dangerous situation. What if they try to starve us, the way the Prussians did in 1870? It was horrible. Every day someone died of hunger. I honestly don't know what we should do. It could be just as dangerous to travel to the north."

"We will remain here, and that's that," said Maman. "Our army will protect us."

The pilot continued to appear at six each evening. People peered from their windows, stood on their balconies, and even gathered in clusters on the street below to see the German aviator flying over Paris in his Taube aircraft. On September 2 he was not alone in the sky. French planes chased him and fired upon him, but he must have been flying too high and beyond their reach. No one brought him down.

Guy watched with fascination and a secret wish that he could fly a plane and chase this pilot back to Germany or wherever he came from. The next day the German aviator receded into the background. Something else was happening. Flyers were all over the place, and on them was printed a letter from the governor general, General Galliéni. He was to be in control of Paris now. A general, not the president or the prime minister, or even the deputies. They and most of the government of France were on their way to Bordeaux.

It was true then. The German army was ready to attack Paris. The citizens would have to fight to defend themselves.

The German pilot would not be part of that invasion. He was found near the Bois de Vincennes in his aircraft. The newspaper story said that he had died from a bullet wound to the heart. His plane had managed to set down lightly on the ground without crashing.

"I'm sorry that he's dead," Guy told Sarah and Maman.

Maman shook her head in disbelief. "But he was dropping bombs on us!"

13

THE DECISION: 1915

With the menace of attack, Paris became a dark and gloomy place. The streets were empty. Now there were no taxis left in the city, horse drawn or motor powered. They had all been ordered to transport soldiers to the battlefront. From dawn to dusk on September 7, six hundred taxis drove back and forth to the front twice, each time with ten soldiers aboard.

Many shop windows were boarded up, or there was a sign announcing that the owner was now a soldier, or that he had died on the field of honor, which meant that he had been killed in action. No one could go out at night because of the curfew, and the days were anxious ones. Guy could feel the tension as all Paris waited for the siege to begin or for the Germans to invade their city. They would fight the enemy just as they had fought the floods four years ago. They would unite to save their city.

But the attack never came. Instead, the French army rallied to attack the Germans. They succeeded in chasing the Germans back beyond their lines. After the Miracle of the Marne, Parisians could go about their business again. The papers never said how many soldiers died or were wounded, but Guy thought that if it had been a real miracle, there would have been few casualties and the army would not be calling up more men.

Guy's oral exam was postponed indefinitely. He had heard nothing from the School of Fine Arts and didn't even return to ask about his application. Monsieur Bresson would probably just wave his hands and blame the war.

By Christmas it was clear that the war would not be over soon. The armies appeared to be stuck. The Germans could not advance any closer to France, and the French couldn't make the Germans go away. Both armies, as well as the English, who were fighting with the French, had dug ditches in the earth—long, deep ditches. Guy had heard that the trenches, for that is what they were called, went all the way from Belgium to Switzerland. The French soldiers and the German soldiers lived in these trenches, and even though they attacked each other from time to time, neither side could dislodge the other from these deep, damp shelters in the mud.

Papa was turned down again by the army. In February, Guy told his family that he couldn't wait any longer. He couldn't stand by and do nothing while others were fighting to protect him and his family and his city. "I'll be nineteen in April. Before they call me up, I'm going to enlist."

Papa didn't say anything about Guy's being an impetuous young man.

Although Maman was not joyful, she admitted, "Guy will be called up soon." Under her breath she murmured, "I'm so afraid this war will last a long time."

When Guy came home in his pale blue jacket, oversized gray overcoat, and red trousers, Sarah did not fuss over him. "What if Willy has become a soldier too? Have you thought of that, Guy? How can you fight Willy?" she said.

"Sarah," Papa said sternly. "Think about what you are saying. We are at war with Austria."

"I'm not," she said.

"I'm not at war with Willy," Guy said. "We will always be friends, no matter what happens. But I have a duty to my country. My responsibility is to fight as a soldier. And Willy must do the same. There are thousands and thousands of soldiers, Sarah. Willy and I will never meet. The Austrians will be fighting in the east—surely."

"How can you be so sure?" Sarah said.

"Because I have to be," Guy said softly.

On the day that Guy left for training, Maman, Papa, and Sarah went with him to the station. He kissed them good-bye and boarded the train. It was filled with recruits and volunteers. He sat beside a young man from Passy named Etienne. He too had joined before he was to be called up. He was a student in a Protestant seminary, but he told Guy that he couldn't study in calm and security while other young men must fight to defend France.

Guy understood what he meant. He felt the same way about painting. No matter how much he loved painting, there was something more important that he must do first. Guy's mind was clear. He knew now who he was. He was a soldier.

14

DRILL AND FIRE: 1915

My dear sister Sarah,

I hope that Papa and Maman and you are all well. Apart from being hungry all the time, I am fine. Every day we are up at dawn in our uniforms, and then we march all morning with a 24-kilo knapsack loaded on our backs. We march and drill and shoot and dig holes in the ground. Just holding my monstrously long rifle requires all my strength, let alone trying to shoot it. I have become quite strong–you wouldn't recognize me. We "blues," as the new soldiers are called, marched 10 kilometers day before yesterday. We made such good time that the corporal was impressed enough to give us the next afternoon off.

The others went fishing, but I made sketches to send to you.

I won't bother to tell you the name of the village. We're not supposed to give such details in our letters, and even if I did, it would be marked out by the censor. Anyway, this is the village. We are camped just outside it on a farm. The officers sleep in a room in the farmhouse, and the rest of us sleep in our sleeping bags on a sheet of canvas on the ground.

There are sketches, too, of some of the men in our section—some are farmers, some come from Paris, and there is even an old man, every bit of thirty-nine, a saddle maker from Rouen. He's very tough and exceedingly strong. We call him Pépère because he looks out for us like a grandfather. The younger man is Etienne. I met him on the train. He plans to be a missionary in Africa. He is obviously a better student than I could ever have been and knows a lot about music too. Willy would like him, I think.

I did a sketch of Willy too. It's from memory and my imagination. I think I know what his uniform looks like. But I don't know if Willy looks the same. I doubt if I do.

I have heard a rumor—we will be leaving for the front soon. That is all I know.

I have written Maman and Papa, of course, but please do not tell them everything that I tell you. I don't want to upset them in any way. No bad news, if you understand.

Thank you for the cakes and sausage. Take good care of Maman and Papa and say a prayer for me. And please write. I cannot be sure your letters will reach me. It is even harder to know if mine will reach you. But I do read all your letters that come. They remind me of the happiness we have shared.

Your loving brother,

Guy

Guy knew it would be useless to write to Willy. But he thought often about his friend. They were both soldiers now. Willy's days were probably much the same as Guy's. Six or seven weeks of camping, marching, camping, moving. Guy began to wonder if they would ever engage the enemy, if the rumor was true. At last the order came for the company to move to the front. Now there would be a purpose to their drilling and marching.

They marched all day in a drizzle of rain. The road turned to mud beneath their boots and made the going slippery. The fields and villages had been the scene of heavy fighting in September. Guy saw with his own eyes the cost of the victory of the Marne. Empty shell cases littered the muddy field, and here and there water pooled in the craters made by mortars. Wooden crosses dotted the fields where fallen soldiers had been buried. The crosses were the only sign of the soldiers who had given their lives to push the Germans back and save Paris from attack.

The villages had all been heavily bombarded. Piles of shattered stone surrounded the walls of the few houses and shops left standing. Guy stared at a two-story house that was completely open on one side, like a dollhouse. The wall had been blown off, and Guy could see on one floor a table and chairs, and upstairs a bed and table. How strange that the wall had been blown away and yet the mirror in the bedroom was not shattered. Guy looked away, feeling uncomfortable about invading the privacy of a family's house.

As they marched, they passed soldiers who had already fought, the soldiers they would replace. Guy tried to remember their faces so that he could sketch them later. Their uniforms were bloody and torn, many with burn holes in them. Their faces were mud covered and haggard. Many were bandaged and limped or walked with their rifles as canes. One wounded soldier shouted, "Courage!" as he passed them.

That night they slept in a barn and rose early the next morning to march to Revigny and pack into a train. They rode crushed together in cattle cars for hours, and when night came they slept in the train. Finally the next morning they jumped from the train and headed deeper into the region, where fighting was going on.

They reached the outer edge of the war zone, where camps were set up like temporary towns for soldiers. Food supplies, munitions, horses, and medicine arrived almost daily. The wounded were treated in tent hospitals here until they could be taken to a hospital in a town or city. Soldiers rested and ate and waited. At least that's what Pépère said.

He explained that they were on the outskirts of the combat zone. "But that doesn't mean a shell won't land on you. We're shelling them right back, you can be sure. Hear the guns? That's our artillery."

Guy wasn't sure at first which guns belonged to their side and which to the Germans. He could hear the rumble of guns firing, and the sound of shells hitting the earth and exploding was steady, if muffled. Then he realized that he could feel the vibrations of the French artillery from his feet to his stomach to his head.

Soon enough he actually saw the French guns. The order came to chase some German soldiers from a village up ahead. The enemy had succeeded in breaking through the lines and now occupied a bombed-out village. On their way to the village, which was between the first and second line of trenches, they passed the big guns. Guy watched the artillerymen fire the 75-millimeter cannons. An officer stood on a wooden trestle and barked out commands to a team of four soldiers. They loaded the huge shells into the chamber, stepped back, and fired. Again and again and again. Every three seconds. They worked like mechanical men at top speed. The explosions were constant and deafening. Guy would never forget what a seventy-five sounded like.

They moved forward, away from the artillery and toward the enemy. At last they came to trenches near the village of Roclincourt, a curving line of deep ditches, several meters deep. They climbed down ladders to get into the trenches, and from below Guy could look up and see only the sky. Wood platforms had been erected for sentinels to keep watch over the front. Here the explosions were much louder. Guy heard shells whistle overhead too, and he wondered how safe they were with no shelter over their heads, no matter how deep the ditches were.

After moving along in the trenches, they climbed out onto the ground. The air was charged with energy. Guy felt a surge of excitement–and anxiety too. Cannon fire rumbled in the distance. The explosions grew louder and sharper as they marched toward the sound. A steady pace. No one spoke. The *tramp, tramp, tramp* of their steps filled Guy's ears like a chant. He felt he didn't exist anymore. Not a single soldier did. They had become a giant animal moving on a thousand legs toward the enemy.

An exploding shell ripped through the air and crashed into the trees beside them. The corporal roared an order and they strung out in two thin lines heading toward what was left of a sparse woods before them. A few trees with leaves and branches stood among the blackened stumps. Guy saw smoke rising in black puffs

from the village. He couldn't remember the name of the village. Was it Neuville? Which Neuville? All he remembered was that they were going to attack the Germans who occupied the village.

Guy dashed with his fellow soldiers from tree to tree, from stump to shrub. They kept low, with their rifles ready to fire at the edge of the crumbling walls of the village. The corporal's order sent the first group of soldiers charging toward it. Guy waited with the second group to cover their attack. Alert in every nerve, Guy watched as his fellow soldiers entered the village. Shots rang out from the village, and the soldiers flattened. Guy aimed and fired in the direction of the shots. Then silence, in which he could hear his heart beating. He could smell damp leaves, smoke, and gunpowder all mixed together. Rain that had fallen for days chilled the air, but sweat dripped from his face. He listened for rifle fire but heard only the rumbling of distant cannons that had begun to fire again.

The signal came. It was their turn to rush the village. Guy burst into movement as he and his comrades surged through the village. German soldiers fired at them, and they shot back, but the Germans were on the run.

They were retreating from the village. Ahead of him down a narrow street Guy saw a group of five or six Germans. Guy noted their gray uniforms and spiked helmets as he scrambled for cover. They fired, then ducked behind a pile of rubble. Guy crouched at the edge of a blown-out building.

An enemy soldier rose to fire and was struck by a bullet. His rifle thudded onto the cobblestone street as he fell. More shots rang out from the Germans, and a French soldier behind Guy crumpled to the ground. Guy stood to fire quickly toward the Germans, then crouched again, waiting. Again and again he fired and crouched. Then silence. He waited, then peered from behind the building. No one fired. He stood but drew no fire. The shooter had gone, or he was dead.

The soldiers from his section appeared everywhere. They had retaken the village. But there was no time to rejoice. The corporal praised them, then ordered them back to their camp. "This was only a detour. We'll get back on track tomorrow."

Guy looked for Etienne, but he didn't find him. That night he waited for a long time beside Etienne's tent, but he never showed up.

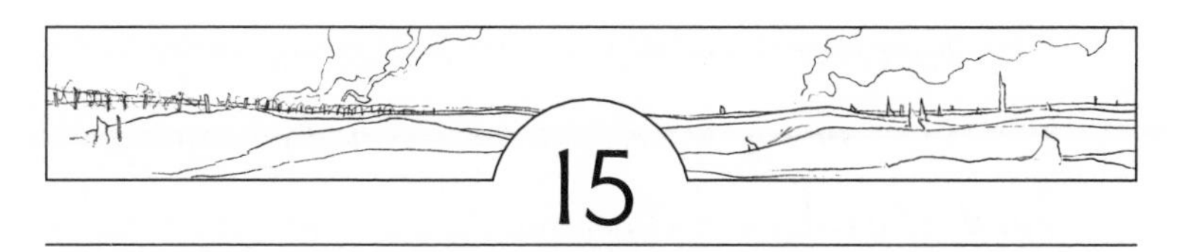

15

THE TRENCHES: SPRING, SUMMER, FALL 1915

Dear Sarah,

I am writing from the front-line trenches. We've been here for almost two weeks, since we moved up from the base camp. We marched from camp, deposited the artillery, and then came to the "deluxe" trenches. I call them that because they are not the messy, chopped-up ditches we live in now. The trenches farther from the front line have wooden planks to walk on when it rains and ladders to climb up and down from the depths. There are platforms, too, where we stand and watch to see if the enemy are trying to sneak into the front-line trenches.

We have come up here to relieve the men who

have been here for over a month. We eat and sleep in this long, snaking trench. We haven't had rain for a couple of weeks, so it isn't slippery and muddy, but it gets hot during the day and the stench–. Well, I'll leave that to your imagination. Except there is no way anyone can imagine such a smell. You have to experience it firsthand to believe it.

We are dug in on one side and the Germans on the other. Great loops of barbed wire stretch beyond the trenches to keep the enemy out. Then right in the middle between us lies an empty field. Crops must have grown here at one time, or pasture. I can see something green trying to grow again in spots, but it doesn't stand a chance. Not with the shelling that goes on. Sometimes we cut the wire and slip across. We scout to see if we can see what damage our bombs have done, or we try to capture Germans and bring them back to question them. Or we attack. I haven't actually done that yet, but I know that one night I will.

Cannons rumble day and night, from both directions. Deep bass groans, then whistling sounds, and blasts when they strike the earth, the earth or something softer. The most amazing thing though, Sarah, is that in the brief silences I have heard larks singing. They go about their business in no-man's-land as if they weren't right in the middle of two warring armies.

I hope you are all well. I know you will be pleased to know that I have been granted leave soon and will be coming home to visit. Thank you for sending the food packages and for the Jules Verne book. I would like to be with the characters in the book, flying around the world in a balloon. After soup and beans and a mystery stew, I am grateful for all the food you send me.

Your loving brother,

Guy

When Guy returned to Paris, his family treated him like a king.

Maman kept asking him, "Wouldn't you like more to eat? Have another piece of pie." She must have asked him a hundred times if he was comfortable.

Papa listened to what Guy said about the war as if he were a distinguished professor giving a lecture. Their attention made him feel like a guest, even a bit like a stranger.

Guy slept much of the time. Often he woke in the middle of the night. He expected the flash, boom, and crash of mortar fire, but instead, silence. It must have been the silence that woke him.

Sarah was especially kind. She acted as if she understood that Guy didn't want to talk about all of the details of his life as a soldier. Hadn't he already written her from the front?

Before he left, she said, "In a way I am jealous of you, Guy. Somehow in your horrible trenches, you are so much closer to Willy than I can ever be. You know what it is like to be a soldier. All I can do is knit scarves and gloves for the soldiers."

She meant close in spirit, not in body. Guy hoped that he never came physically close to Willy during the war.

And then it was time to return, time to become a soldier again. Back at the base camp the memory of his visit home faded quickly. Had he really slept in a comfortable bed and eaten meals served on china plates, or had it all been a dream?

Pépère told him he had missed a raid, one by the

Germans. It had been at new moon. The enemy had crawled across no-man's-land and managed to cut through the barbed wire and toss hand grenades into the trenches. "You won't recognize the place. I was nearly buried by the side of the trench, and two were crushed in the worthless wooden bomb shelter, but we stopped them all right. They didn't get the prisoners they were looking for." Pépère added, "We're heading back up there in a few days."

The day Guy's unit was ordered back to the trenches, it stormed. At least the rain cooled them off. They marched through the mud to the even muddier trenches. They reached the trenches farthest from the first line and climbed down into the soggy ditches. To reach the first line they wended their way through communication trenches that joined the two lines of trenches. The familiar whistle of falling shells and constant drumming of the guns grew louder. They passed muddy, exhausted soldiers returning, and finally they reached their destination.

Rainwater pooled at the bottom of the trench. Soldiers had dug cubbyholes in the dirt walls or perched on wooden supports above the filthy water.

Guy slept as well as he could standing on one of these

supports. With relief the next morning he looked up at the strip of blue sky above him. The rain had stopped. Who knows? Maybe they would be dry again. Guy settled back into the curious routine of the trenches. Half of the time he was bored with waiting. The other half, and this was usually at night, he was both tense and excited. Because it was at night they crawled through no-man's-land to spy on the enemy or to attack them.

Every time Guy went out, he wondered if he would come back alive. Was it possible for a person to know in advance if he would die? Guy thought it might be, and you didn't even have to be a soldier to know. Hadn't Willy's mother known, the summer before she died? Isn't that why she wanted Willy to be with her all the time? She must have known that was her last summer on earth. Guy himself never felt sure of anything. That uncertainty gave him hope and fear at the same time–hope that he would come back, and fear that he would be killed.

One evening in the early fall Guy waited with Pépère for the darkness of night. Their corporal had chosen twenty of them to surprise the Boche in an evening raid. Rumors had been flying that the Germans were moving around, that maybe they were planning a major assault.

The shelling had slowed down, and the machine gun that usually rattled directly across from them was silent. Had the gunner left, or was it a trick? They were going to find out. But not until dark.

Guy's mind filled with thoughts while he waited, thoughts of how the war had changed everything. If it weren't for the war, he and Willy would have been together. Then Willy would have come home with him and stayed with his family. Now they were enemy soldiers, carrying guns and living in a world of trenches and bombardments, of fighting and death. He could never have imagined such a war. No one could have.

Corporal Terrier ordered his men out into the night. Guy and Pépère slid under the barbed wire with the other soldiers. Bright stars shone indifferently in a clear sky. A rumbling like thunder grew louder. A menacing hum sounded above and a shell fired by German artillery exploded in the French trench not thirty meters from where they crawled out. Guy hesitated. Should they return and find out if anyone had been hit? He could see soldiers from his patrol inching across no-man's-land. He followed them. Shells continued to strike the ground and explode. It didn't sound as if the enemy had pulled away from their trenches. They were as menacing as ever.

Smoke blotted the stars. On his stomach Guy tried to move faster, digging in with his elbows and knees. Machine-gun fire rattled above them. Guy flattened and crawled into a shell crater beneath the range of the machine gun. Amidst the rapid firing he heard a cry; then someone said, "It's Louis. I'll see to him."

Guy strained to see in the darkness. Then a flare flashed in the distant sky and he saw someone crouched over and running like a crab. It was someone from their patrol, and he was hurrying toward a soldier lying face-down with his arms stretched out in front of him. Louis. The soldier remained crouched beside Louis for a few seconds; then he set off, crawling, toward the German trench.

Guy realized there was nothing the soldier could do for Louis. They would carry his body back on their return. Guy crawled from the shell hole and made his way toward a huge coil of barbed wire. It had already been cut, and carefully he crawled through the opening as bullets whizzed above them.

Guy heard a gruff voice in the darkness. "My turn first." It was Pépere.

A few moments later a grenade exploded in the enemy trench just ahead of him. Pépere must have thrown it. The explosion shook the ground under Guy. Shouts and cries of pain rose in the smoke.

When the smoke cleared, Guy strained to see his fellow soldiers. Had they already attacked, following the grenade? But in what direction? Maybe they were circling back already, or forging ahead. He changed direction and headed to his left. He was pretty sure the enemy trenches were on his right now. The screaming whistle of a shell froze his heart. It was falling near, very near.

Guy rolled into a trench. He fell onto a soldier's body. No movement, no sound came from the body beneath him. Guy covered his head with his arms as the shell exploded not ten meters from the trench. Mud flew into the air. Shrapnel thudded on the ground and landed in the trench.

Then for a moment it was calm. Guy heard a groan across from him. Every cell in his body sprang to life. He stared at a pile of two or three German soldiers lying twisted and still on the bottom of the trench. The pile heaved, and from beneath the dead, a soldier crawled. Coughing and groaning, he rose to his knees. Guy had never been this close to an enemy soldier before–not a live soldier. The soldier slouched toward him. Guy drew his knife and held his breath. Then a flare flashed through the sky, lighting up the trench. The soldier's helmet had fallen off, and Guy could see his face, pale beneath splotches of mud and blood. He was close enough to look into the young man's eyes, dark eyes, deep set and almond shaped, eyes filled with pain. Eyes like Willy's.

Guy dropped his knife. He crawled toward the wounded soldier and held out his arms. The German collapsed against Guy's chest, and Guy tried to hold him up. The rumble of guns grew louder. The French artillery had begun to fire in this direction. It was answered a few seconds later by the German guns. Guy dragged the soldier from the trench, lifted him onto his shoulder, and stumbled, crouching, through no-man's-land. He trudged closer and closer to the whirls of barbed wire in front of the French lines. He reached the wire, dropped down, and laid the soldier on the ground before him. He would crawl under and drag the soldier with him. Then a mortar exploded. Guy threw himself over the soldier. Pieces of metal and mud, rock and dirt, blasted in all directions. He felt shrapnel pierce his shoulder and legs before he lost consciousness.

16

THE MEDAL: OCTOBER 1915

Guy woke up in a bed. He was lying on his side facing a wall. He didn't know where he was or how long he had been in this bed, facing this wall. He started to roll on his back and a sharp pain forced him to stay on his side. He could see peeling green paint on the wall before him. He glimpsed a nurse scurrying past the foot of his bed from time to time. Then pain claimed his attention. His left thigh throbbed, and a flame seemed to sear his back and left shoulder. The pain would not stop. It would not go away. He was glad to be alive, but he wasn't sure he could live with such pain.

Then he heard the sound of marching boots. Was he dreaming? How could this be? *Tramp, tramp, tramp,*

tramp, the steps grew louder. The boots stopped at the foot of his bed. He strained to look up and saw a general standing above him. The general cast off his black cape. A soldier beside him took it and draped it at the foot of Guy's bed.

The general strode to Guy's side and announced, "Guy Masson, for your valor in combat and your service to the Republic of France, I award you the Military Cross. I congratulate you upon your courage. You are an inspiration to our soldiers." He pinned the medal on Guy's pillow, then bent over swiftly and kissed him on the side of his head. Guy noticed the shining gold oak leaf on the general's kepi, his carefully trimmed mustache, and his stern gray eyes.

Guy tried to speak. He opened his mouth and heard a strange growling sound in his throat. In his mind he was saying, "But I don't want this medal," but the only sounds he made were groans.

The general held up his white-gloved hands to calm Guy. Then he returned to the foot of the bed and donned his cape with aid of the soldier beside him, and they both strode from Guy's sight. A few minutes after the general had left, Guy was able to speak.

"No!" he murmured at first. Then his voice grew stronger. "No! No! I won't have it. I don't want this medal." He struggled to remove the medal from the pillow slip, but the pain in his shoulder stopped him.

A nurse hurried to his side. "Don't trouble yourself, monsieur. You must lie still for now. Let's leave the medal there for your family to see. They are coming to the field hospital this afternoon."

Guy felt her tuck the sheet tightly around him. "Now try to sleep, try to rest."

My family? he thought. What family? He tried to remember his mother and father. What did they look like? And his sisters and brothers? Did he have any? Guy let his head sink back onto the pillow and fell almost instantly asleep.

When he woke, a young woman stood beside his bed. She had a frizzle of red curls framing her face, and intense hazel eyes.

"It's Sarah, your sister," she said, and began to cry.

Blinking back tears, she said softly, "It's all right now. You're alive, Guy. Oh, I hope you are not in great pain." After a few moments she took out a handkerchief and blew her nose and dabbed at her eyes. "I'll go get Maman and Papa. We've been standing here watching you sleep for the longest time. I told them to sit down for a while. I'll be right back."

Guy reached out with his hand and Sarah grasped it. He felt the warmth and pressure of her two hands around his, and he knew she was real and he remembered that he had a sister named Sarah.

He closed his eyes for a moment and other images invaded his mind. The patrol in the dark night, crawling across no-man's-land, the grenade in the trench, the mortar fire and explosions, and the enemy soldier. He could see the young soldier's face, his fearful dark eyes.

Guy looked up at Sarah. "I saved Willy, Sarah," he murmured.

"Willy?" Sarah asked. "Did you see him? Where is he?"

"He was wounded, and I dragged him back, and then—" Guy couldn't remember what happened after that. "But where is he? I want to know where he is. Can you find Willy, Sarah?"

"Yes, Guy. Of course I will. But now I'm going to find Maman and Papa." She slipped her hands from his and smiled at him, then turned and walked away.

Guy closed his eyes, and when he opened them,

he saw Maman in her best brown suit and pearl necklace. Papa stood a little behind her, and Sarah was at his side. "Thank God you are alive," Maman said, and kissed him.

Papa smiled, but his eyes filled with tears. He swallowed, then spoke. "I'm proud of you, Guy." He slipped his fingers under the medal fastened to Guy's pillow. "You'll come home soon. You're going to get well, completely well, and come home. We miss you."

The next time Guy's family came to visit, Sarah told him that she had asked about Willy. "Guy, it wasn't Willy. You saved a German soldier. The nurse told me he is much improved. She didn't know what would happen to him."

"But it was Willy. I saw his face."

"Maybe he looked like Willy, but he is a German soldier. His name is Erik Junger. The guard told me he is a prisoner of war and that when he's well, he will work on a farm here in France. With their husbands in the army, women are trying to keep up the farms, but they need help. The guard said there is no more room in the prisons."

Why would Sarah make up such a story? It must be true, Guy thought. If it had been Willy, she would have acted differently. She would have been excited to tell him Willy was alive. "I wish I had saved Willy," he said.

"Then he would be working on a farm here in France," Sarah added.

"It would be better for him," said Guy. "I wish, I wish–"

"We'll find him when the war is over."

Guy didn't believe the war would ever end, or that they would ever see Willy again, but he couldn't say this to Sarah. Instead he just smiled.

17

THE SEARCH FOR WILLY: 1917...

From the field hospital Guy was transferred to a hospital where he had several operations. He recovered from the surgery and went to a sanitarium near Paris. It was actually a château, a stately house that a wealthy man had offered to the nation for use by recovering soldiers. A house and several outbuildings stood on the property, with ponds and gardens and a shabby lawn that had once been well tended.

Guy shared a room with a soldier who had lost his sight. Often Guy read to him from a book that Sarah had brought. "To change your ideas," she had said when she offered him Jules Verne's book about a voyage to the moon. "And because you are such a dreamer."

Reading to the blinded soldier, Guy was grateful that he could see, that his eyes had been spared. Although he would limp all his life and would have pain from the pieces of metal the doctors couldn't remove from his back, he could see.

But he thought there might be something wrong with his brain. He couldn't remember images and details the way he used to. When he sketched, he would draw only what was in front of him, not the fleeting visions he had.

Dr. Nivelle reassured him. "In time your brain will be back to normal."

"And then I will go back to the front."

Dr. Nivelle shrugged. "We will see."

"But I won't kill any enemy soldiers," Guy said. "I have decided not to fight them. I will save them instead. You know, I have already saved an enemy soldier."

"Of course," said Dr. Nivelle.

Guy could see the doubt in the doctor's face. The doctor treated him as if he were a little boy telling a fantastic story. But Guy had thought about what he was saying. To him it made sense.

"Monsieur Masson, you will return to the army only if I pronounce you fit to serve," Dr. Nivelle said. "This war will be over someday," the doctor continued. "And maybe it will take that long for your brain to return to normal."

When Guy was able to walk, he made his way to a chair in the grounds and sat and stared at the pond. Sometimes he took his sketch pad. He would lift it to draw a bird or a flower, then let it fall back onto his lap and stare at the water. He saw sailboats skimming across the pond–red and blue model boats. He thought of Willy. Then he blinked and the sailboats were gone and the pond surface was still.

His parents and Sarah came as often as they could. Papa complained about business, that there was no business. People aren't reading books anymore. All they want to read is the newspapers.

Maman began almost every sentence, "When you come home." Then she took his hand and sighed, and Guy saw tears fill her eyes.

Guy listened to them, reassured by their familiar voices, but sometimes he didn't know what to say, and his thoughts drifted.

Sarah called out, "Guy! Dear, dear Guy. You are on the moon with your mind far away."

The waters of his mind rippled, and he came back to

the surface and listened to Papa read from the newspaper and Maman say, "When you come home."

Sarah tried to cheer him up. She would sit with him for hours and tell him stories from Bregenz.

"Remember when we tried to take Willy home with us? The summer we met him. You drilled holes in Maman's trunk so he could breathe, and Maman found his cap."

"She found his flute too." The image of the trunk suddenly flashed in Guy's mind. "You tried to play his flute, Sarah. You made a dreadful sound with it."

Sarah frowned. "When was it that we made the glider? We worked so hard on it. You went first and then Willy crashed it."

"And broke his wrist, and we were afraid his mother would never let us see him again."

"He was going to play for the emperor."

Like playful streams from a waterfall, Guy's memories poured over him. Talking to Sarah always made him feel better.

By the time Guy was well enough to leave the sanitarium, people were tired of the war. They no longer shouted victory cheers and said that it would be over soon. It had gone on for over three years. Everyone knew someone who had died. They wanted life to return to normal, and in many ways it did. Then a zeppelin would fly above Paris and drop bombs on people and houses as if to say, "You think you are safe far behind the trenches, but see what we can do."

At home Guy tried to focus on his painting. He painted flowers and vases and teapots and pictures of happy times before the war. He painted anything that would help him forget about exploding shells and pain and death.

Then in June 1917 soldiers from the United States arrived to fight on the side of France and England, and before a year and a half passed, the war had ended. The armies tried to count the dead, the wounded, the lost, but it would take years. They would never know for certain how many millions died. On the day the Germans surrendered, the streets of Paris rang with people's shouts.

"They aren't shouting because of our victory," Guy said to Sarah. "They are celebrating the end of the war."

On November 11, 1918, the warring countries signed

an armistice. The newspapers were full of the story. Soon all of the heads of state would be coming to France to draw up the treaty and sign it.

"Now that it's over, Guy, do you think we can find Willy?"

"We will try."

They didn't know where to begin. The war had changed everything. The Austrian Empire was no more. The newspapers reported that people in the defeated cities were dying now from disease and starvation, so even if Willy had survived the war . . .

The thought that haunted Guy was that Willy was dead, and gradually he let Sarah take over the search. If Willy is somehow still alive, he will reach us, Guy thought. We are here in Paris where we have always been. If he doesn't reach us, it is because he is no longer alive.

But Sarah was hopeful. She wrote letters to Willy and to his father. Not one of her letters was answered. They weren't even returned. "It's because of the stupid blockade. The war is over. Why can't we all live together again?"

Papa tried hard to get Guy involved in the publishing business. Guy made an effort to learn how to design and lay out books. Sometimes he drew pictures for advertisements, but the work didn't interest him.

Papa must have noticed how bored Guy was. He suggested one day, "Maybe you should see what has happened at the School of Fine Arts since the war."

Guy hesitated. He had wanted to study there before the war, but it didn't seem important anymore. What could the professors teach now? The world had changed. People wanted to look to the future, not the past, after the war. How many professors would be left, anyway? No, he decided to teach himself, to learn on his own. All he needed was time.

In the spring Guy asked Papa if he could go to Grand-maman's old farmhouse in Normandy. "I can fix it up."

"Excellent idea," Papa agreed. "We could go there for vacation again after all these years."

"Do you want to come with me, Sarah?" Guy asked.

"I'd like to be with you, Guy, but my exam is in June. I've already had to wait too long, and I'm determined to pass my baccalaureate."

Guy went alone to Normandy. He worked hard to restore Grand-maman's old house. He swept and cleaned the inside and repaired and painted the shutters.

He tilled the garden again and planted vegetables and herbs. The apple trees needed pruning, and he spent hours outside sawing dead branches. He didn't mind mucking out the barn and even bought chickens from a neighbor.

In spite of all of the work, he made time for sketching and painting. His favorite time of day was evening, when he would try to capture the golden tinge of light in the sky and the deep green of the thick grass. If his mind wandered to the trenches, to the endless explosions and the bodies of men and horses, he would quickly replace the terrible images with a picture of the stone house or ripening apples.

He looked forward to Sarah's letters and wished she would write more often. How could she possibly have time when she had to study for her exam? With the thought of her upcoming test, he sent her encouraging notes and asked her to come to Normandy as soon as she passed the exam. "We can celebrate your great success," he wrote. Guy had no doubt that Sarah would be brilliant.

For two weeks he heard nothing. Was there a postal strike? he wondered. One afternoon late in July, he glanced out the kitchen window and thought he saw a soldier riding a bicycle up the narrow road to the house. A sudden chill ran through his body as if he were watching a ghost. Then he realized that the man in uniform was not a soldier. He was a postman. At last, a letter from Sarah.

Guy hurried to the front door, threw it open, and waited for the man to arrive. When Guy saw the telegram in the man's hands, his heart beat faster. What could be so urgent?

He tore open the envelope and read the brief message:

Why no answer to my letter

Arriving tomorrow for celebration

Love Sarah

"This is great news!" Guy shouted to the man in uniform.

"Pleased to hear that, monsieur," the man responded and mounted his bike.

Before he could ride off, Guy asked, "There hasn't been a strike, has there? I was expecting a letter before now."

"We do our best, monsieur," the man said as he rode off. "We all do our best."

Guy set to work immediately. Perhaps Maman and

Papa would be coming too—if Papa could get away. He reread the telegram, but Sarah hadn't said. At least he was certain that his sister would be here. He had house-cleaning to do, laundry as well, and he would have to ride to the market in the village.

The next day, midafternoon, all was ready for Sarah. She hadn't arrived yet. To make the time go faster, Guy set up his easel in the garden near the apple tree he had been painting. Soon he was concentrating on recreating on his canvas the green-gold of a ripening apple. Again and again he mixed yellow and blue paint on his palette, trying to find the exact color. When he did, he brushed it within the outline of the apple on his canvas.

"Guy! Guy! We're here!"

He glanced up over the top of his canvas when he heard Sarah's voice. He saw her waving as she stood by the corner of the house. She was not alone.

Guy put his palette down and stood up. Sarah hurried toward Guy, and her straw hat flew off her head. The man bent down and grabbed the hat in his left hand. He stood up and waved the hat at Guy. And Guy saw that the empty right sleeve of the man's coat was pinned to his chest.

A soldier, he thought. He has given his arm for his country. And then he recognized the man.

"Guy, Guy, Willy has found us!" Sarah rushed up to Guy, then kissed him on both cheeks.

In a moment Willy was beside her, and Guy reached out to grasp his friend's left hand.

"Guy." Willy paused. His wide smile made his eyes crinkle shut. "I've asked Sarah to marry me."

Speechless with joy, Guy stood for a moment looking at Willy and Sarah. Then he said, "Now we will be brothers."

AUTHOR NOTE

The characters in this story are fictional, as are the specific details of their experiences and actions. I have placed them in an actual period of history during which many of the events mentioned in the story did occur. The 1910 flood was one of the worst in Paris history. When the Eiffel Tower was built for the Universal Exposition in Paris in 1889, it was not a popular monument. In fact, the writers Emile Zola and Guy de Maupassant were among three hundred who signed a petition protesting the construction of the "useless and monstrous Eiffel Tower." Many Parisians agreed with them. But it survived and proved to be useful for telegraph transmissions and surveillance during World War I, which erupted in Europe in the late summer of 1914. The Great War, as it was then known, soon involved nations in Asia and Africa, as well as the United States, which sent soldiers to fight in June 1917.

A decade earlier, Count Ferdinand von Zeppelin had experimented with hydrogen-filled airships, which he launched over Lake Constance, bordering Switzerland, Germany, and Austria, in the early 1900s. People thought him crazy for attempting to fly such a craft. However, during WWI many zeppelins, by that time helium-filled, were launched and flew over England and Paris to drop bombs on the civilian populations, killing many and terrifying even more. By the time the war ended in 1918, more than 10 million soldiers had died, and another 20 million had been wounded. Uncounted civilians lost their homes and their villages. No statistics exist for the number of civilians who died. It was a brutal and tragic experience in the second decade of a century that had begun with optimism for the future and a belief in progress.

If you would like to read more about this period in history, I recommend that you start with visits to your local library and bookstores. Below are books, films, and websites that have informed and inspired me, and that you might find interesting.

BOOKS

NONFICTION

The Battle of the Marne, Henri Isselin, (translated by Charles Connell), Doubleday & Company, Inc., 1966.

Jacques-Henri Lartigue: Boy with a Camera, John Cech, Four Winds Press, 1994.

Lines of Fire: Women Writers of World War I, edited by Margaret R. Higonnet, Plume/Penguin Putnam, 1999.

Thunder at Twilight, Frederic Morton, Charles Scribner's Sons, 1989.

The Western Front Illustrated, John Laffin, Grange Books, 1997.

With Those Who Wait, Frances Wilson Huar, George H. Doran Company, 1918.

FICTION

All Quiet on the Western Front, Erich Maria Remarque, translated from the German by A.W. Wheen, Random House, 1996 (originally published in Germany as *Im Westen Nichts Neues,* 1929).

No Hero for the Kaiser, Rudolf Frank, translated by Patricia Crampton, Lothrop, Lee & Shepard, 1986 (originally published in Germany as *Der Schädel des Negerhäuptlings Makaua,* 1932).

War Boy, written and illustrated by Michael Foreman, Arcade, 1994.

FILMS

All Quiet on the Western Front, U.S., 1930, directed by Lewis Milestone.

La Grande Illusion (The Grand Illusion), France, 1937, directed by Jean Renoir.

The Great War and the Shaping of the 20th Century, U.S., 1996, PBS documentary.

La Vie et Rien d'Autre (Life and Nothing But), France, 1989, directed by Jean Tavernier.

Westfront 1918, Germany, 1930, directed by G.W. Pabst.

WEBSITES

http://nosvoyages.free.fr/autrefois/crue_1910/index.htm
Contains photographs taken in Paris during the 1910 flood.

www.nga.gov/resources/expo1889.htm
Contains archive photos of the Universal Exposition in Paris in 1889, featuring the Eiffel Tower.

www.pbs.org/greatwar/
Companion website to the 1996 PBS documentary *The Great War and the Shaping of the 20th Century*.

www.firstworldwar.com/index.htm
Historical website edited by Michael Duffy.